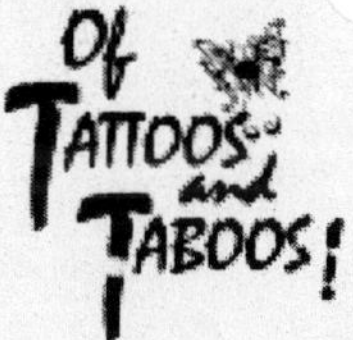

A flight down the forbidden aisles

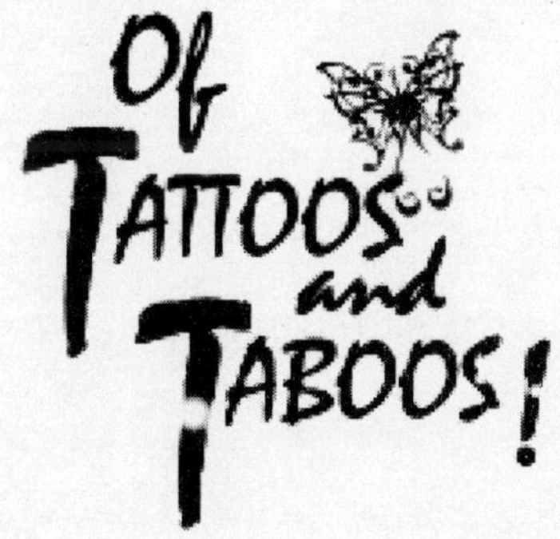

Of Tattoos and Taboos!

A flight down the forbidden aisles

Anurag Anand

Srishti
PUBLISHERS & DISTRIBUTORS

Srishti Publishers & Distributors
N-16, C. R. Park
New Delhi 110 019
srishtipublishers@gmail.com

First published by Srishti Publishers & Distributors in 2012

All the characters and incidences described in this book are a work of pure fiction. Any resemblance to any person dead or alive is purely coincidental.

Typeset in AGaramond 12pt. by Suresh Kumar Sharma at Srishti

Printed and bound in India

For Parents, the most selfless and doting amongst all of God's creations!

Wandering aimlessly in the maze of life,
An illuminated path I stumbled upon.
Fragrant and beckoning, like the meadows of spring,
For once I knew where I wanted to sing.

Basking, as I perched upon the wuthering heights,
In my clouded wit a sudden thought dawned.
Your prayers were always my guiding light,
In their simmering incense I found my flight.

The rebukes and the slap on my little wrists,
The pat on my back that I so much relished,
Were fragments of a greater design I now see,
For this is where you had always willed for me to be.

Authors Note

From the few characters back in college, who could at best be classified as mere acquaintances, one that I clearly remember till date is Prince. His real name I didn't know and never bothered to find out, but it were his mannerisms and conduct that made him peculiar – different from us 'normal' folks and hence a phenomenon to be observed from only a safe distance.

With his shoulder-length hair – sometimes left unkempt and often beaded, denims that survived dangerously – often threatening to slip down and bare the whole of his semi-revealed underpants and the odd assortment of jewelry dangling from the piercings on his earlobes and brows, he was nothing like the boys I preferred to hang out with. He spoke with a confused accent, often rhyming his words and interspersing them with expletives, imitating rap and hip-hop artists with notorious credentials. He was lean and tiny and walked with a swagger, like a dangling vine caught in an autumn breeze.

His peculiarity had prevented me from making any efforts at familiarization and I wasn't sure if he was even aware of my existence until the fateful day when I bumped into him at the Patna railway station. I was on my way back to Delhi after spending the summer break with my grandparents and was waiting for the train, which was delayed by about an hour, when I saw him. He too was at the station, perhaps waiting for the same train and flanked by his parents and a young girl who could have been his younger sister.

What left me shellshocked though, was that Prince nowhere resembled the living bastion of the hip-hop cult that we often saw treading about in the college campus. He was a normal boy, clad in a shirt and a pair of trousers, sans the jewelry, the beads and the accent.

His long hair, the only residue of his alternate identity, was neatly oiled and pulled backwards. His parents too looked like simple folks, the kind that you brush your shoulders against in every street and marketplace of Patna. His sister was clad in a cotton salwar-suit and seemed to be animatedly describing something to her brother. And just when I thought I had seen it all I saw him bend down and touch his parent's feet before getting on to the train.

There was nothing odd about a son seeking his parent's blessings before embarking on a journey and there probably would have been a hundred others emulating the act before the train pulled out from the station. But Prince! Left to me, I would have placed his roots to anywhere in Africa or the Middle East, but certainly not the virtuous state of Bihar. And the same Prince who seemed to preserve not an ounce of respect for anything Indian, touching his parents feet, was like staring at the Seven Wonders of the World, all rolled into one. I was amused and deliberately I even walked past his seat a couple of times during the journey only to be summarily ignored, out of sheer ignorance or a sense of embarrassment, I would never know.

But today when I look around, I see numerous Princes', male and female, leading lives of contrasting duality. The ever increasing rural urban divide has intensified the phenomenon of migration to big cities and those leaving their homes in search of better career opportunities can often be seen changing into completely different individuals in a bid to adapt to their newfound surroundings. In some cases this transition remains superficial, impacting only the exterior façade of the individual in question, whilst for others it ends up becoming an all encompassing transformation of the personality.

What you shall read in the following pages is a similar story of transition - of an innocent small-town girl into a big-city damsel; of values and beliefs into the ruthless instinct for survival; of Sejal Patel into Sherlyn Ahuja. The story, a first person account by the protagonist herself, traces the period of her life and the sequence of events that meticulously chisel her character and individuality until she finds a completely different person staring back at her from the mirror.

Transition is an integral and continual component of all our lives and it is neither advisable nor prudent to resist each of the varied forms of change we encounter. The question that remains then is where should we draw the line? What degree and type of change is acceptable and which of it needs to be resisted?

I hope that 'Of tattoos and Taboos!' meets your expectations and helps you in arriving at the answers to some of these complex questions posed by life.

There are many who have played their parts in ensuring that this book, in its current form, reaches your hands at the earliest and it might be difficult to thank all of them here. However a few names I can't do without mentioning are my wife Neeru and daughter Naisha for their sheer presence in my life – Thank you for being there; Atul, now a colleague, but a guy I know from the time he was still learning to tie his shoelaces for his insightful inputs and encouraging words; and those online friends who have taken the efforts to look me up and add me to their social networks – please keep your comments and feedback trickling as they are the most treasured rewards for my writing.

ONE

A little brown tab was blinking profusely at the base of my laptop screen. With a slight click it expanded into a full fledged chat window concealing half the Word document that I had been intently scrutinizing. 'How are you placed tomorrow evening?' the message from Srini read.

I suppressed the smile that was struggling to emerge on my lips. This was long overdue. I had been expecting the message. 'Nothing much…,' the alphabets sequentially appeared on the screen as my fingers instinctively tapped the reply on the keyboard. I paused, placing my ring finger on the Backspace key and holding it till the screen was clear once again. No, it is too early, I thought to myself.

Once again, my fingers were hammering the keys of the laptop and this time I knew what I was writing. I inspected the message one more time before clicking the Send icon. 'Why? No one home?' my reply read.

'Mansi is traveling for some conference, so it is just me and the kids. It will be nice if you drop by. The kids would like that too,' he responded within a split-second. Once again, expectedly!

The kids, my foot! I knew better than to believe that he was looking to invite a playmate for his kids while their mother was away. But by now I was well versed with the rules of the game - Never make it easy for them. Ignite a flame of hope and just when its warmth starts to spread, extinguish it mercilessly. Go about this routine again and again till you see them huffing, panting and reeling under some invisible cramps.

It was important to maintain the balance though. The teasing had to be just enough to entice frustration but had to cease before the thread of attraction snapped under the weight of despondency and hopelessness. It was only now, after years of relentless practice that I could claim to have mastered the art of manipulating our dear Martians – Men, as you call them.

'Oh… I would have loved to, but had already made a plan to go out with some friends. Can't back out now, but we can catch up one of the days in the following week,' I replied. And to add a flavor of emotions, I added, 'It's been so long since I met the kids. Do pass on my apologies to them.'

I had barely met his kids once - a boy who had just about started walking and a girl who could have been anything between 5 and 7 years of age, during a dinner he had organized for a few of us from work. I didn't even remember their names and the last thing I expected was for them to remember me. He too, I was sure, didn't intend to pass on apologies from a near stranger for not being able to visit them. But I liked the emotional flavor I had introduced into the conversation.

I was smiling to myself as I read his reply, some gibberish about 'being extremely disappointed' and yet 'understanding my prior commitments'. Putting my laptop on standby mode I rummaged through my bag for the pack of cigarettes and lighter I had dumped inside barely an hour back. It was just about time for my next smoking break.

I am Sherlyn Ahuja, Sejal Patel for some, employed as a Marketing Manager with a telecom major in Mumbai. I am a normal girl, just like you or those that you bump into on the crowded streets of the metropolis at an alarming frequency. I am smart, usually well-dressed (unless you have had the privilege of catching me in my pajamas) and if those around me are to be believed, a stunning looker. I would have concurred with my admirers, but for my nose which could have been significantly sleeker and my derriere which could have done without some of its extra padding. But then, don't they say that none of us are perfect?

During my 29 years, life had created ample opportunities to subject me to its throes and each time it latched on to one, it left me better informed and equipped to deal with its vagaries. My most vital erudition pertained to the understanding of men – the way they thought, behaved and reacted - and this clearly was the most invaluable addition to my armory for taking on life, head on.

No wonder they keep harping about the impermeability of a woman's mind. We women have a varied mix of thoughts and emotions that dictate our behavior – our friends, family and loved ones, our ambitions and aspirations, our acquired likes and dislikes, to name a few. And hence, it becomes difficult to identify the right mix of motivators that are at play within us at any given point in time.

In the Hindu epic Ramayana, Kaikeyi, one of the three queens of King Dashrath used the boons she had earned in the battlefield from her husband to further the ascent of her own son Bharath to the throne of Ayodhya. Was her motivation to send Rama, the King's son from another queen, on a fourteen year exile so difficult to understand?

Or, was Cleopatra's alignment with Mark Antony in the wake of Caesar's assassination too difficult to comprehend? History stands witness that women have usually depended on practicality and logic to determine their actions. Occasionally some of them have been steered by the callings of their hearts and their emotions, but those instances too remain perfectly explicable. What then does the near-epical complexity of the female mind owe its origin to?

Relativity! And no, I am not referring to the complex theory of physics associated with one Mister Albert Einstein. My theory is far simpler than that. The thought process of a woman, with its myriad determinants is 'relatively' more complex than that of a man whose actions are usually based around a single motive – sex. Of course there is the unreasonably bloated male ego, but mostly the passage to its gratification also happens to be testosterone infested.

Be it the dresses and perfumes men wear, the vehicles they drive or the career options they choose, the one thing that can definitely be found lurking about in some nook of their mind is a frenzied romp. A cricketer practices for many hours so that some day he gets to don the national colors and get laid along the way, by the girls in college or the neighborhood initially, and ramp-worthy models later in his career.

A film producer makes a movie to entertain his audiences, make money and also warm his couch along the way. An author writes to satisfy his creative urges, engage his readers and hopefully impress some of them enough to lead them to his bedroom. The list is endless. And it is across this common thread that indiscriminately binds all men that I discovered the secret to a happy and fulfilling life.

And before you go about branding me as a slut, let me clarify – I am not a vociferous proponent of promiscuity. In fact I firmly believe in being faithful to one's partner and also in the institution of marriage. Only 'trust' to me is an implicit thing of the mind and not a derivative pegged to random acts of physicality or sensual pleasure.

Confused? Don't be, not just as yet; such reactions are commonplace when it comes to my views on relationships and particularly sex. Some friends have even gone on to call my thinking warped and delusional, but I care two hoots. I have justifications for all my prejudices and actions, but I owe them to none and neither shall I go about boring the shit out of you by narrating them here. Instead, let me take you on a journey through the past few years of my life that resulted in shaping me into what I am today.

TWO

'Sejal… Sejal…,' I could hear Kamini's voice, shrilling as a whistle, even from the confines of my room. I picked up a hand-towel to wipe the extra kohl I had smeared on my eyes, startled by her sudden entry. I wasn't required to answer back and I knew that it wouldn't matter even if I did. She would keep screaming her lungs out as she traced her steps from the hall downstairs through the staircase right up to my room on the first floor.

Just as I dropped the towel on the dressing table, the mirror ahead confirming that I had erased the traces of my friend's intrusion from my face, the door to my room burst open. 'What are you doing? You are still not ready? Hurry up, we are getting late,' Kamini was her usual anxious self as she barged into the room, showering me with a flurry of questions.

Today was the last day of Navratri and like most cities of Gujarat, Rajkot too was bubbling with the last burst of energy before the culmination of nine-day long festivities and months of preceding preparations. For the past eight nights we friends had been attending the Dandia celebrations organized at the Race Course ground near the city center. Our examination results had come out a few months back and the fact that now we were all certified MBAs from the Saurashtra University provided us with yet another reason to celebrate.

Kamini is my neighbor and we have been friends for as long as I can remember. We went to school together then college and we remained together even during our post graduation. In fact I had no inclination to continue with studies after completing my B. Com. Honors and it was only because Kamini was hell bent upon studying further that I too had enrolled myself for the MBA course offered by the Management Faculty of the University.

Rajkot is a small town and most people falling within the same age group know each other from some place or the other – having studied together, attended tuitions together or friends of friends and so on. Barring the few who had come from interiors of Saurashtra to the city in pursuit of higher education, most of our MBA batch comprised of people we knew beforehand. As a result, the two years we spent at the university were filled with casual banter, fun and frolic and it was only when the dates for the final examinations were announced that we woke up to the inevitable end of the happy times.

Only a handful of our classmates were intending to put their newly acquired degrees to use and had started applying for jobs in the larger cities - Ahmedabad and Mumbai. The rest were either undergoing induction into their family businesses or were skimming through the numerous marital alliances their parents were busy accumulating. I, once again, found myself in a zone of confusion and directionlessness.

'Didn't I tell you, yellow is your color! You are looking fabulous,' I complemented Kamini on the Ghaghara Choli that I had helped her pick. 'Yes, it's looking nice isn't it? But is the necklace matching? See!' she was now posing, neck craned, expecting me to comment on the hideocity curled around it . 'Here, see if these look any better,' I said, handing her the bead necklace that I had intended to wear myself. After all it was an extremely important day for her and it was imperative that she be at her best.

Kamini was the first amongst us to have a boyfriend - Nirav our classmate from college. It was sometime during the second year that they started seeing each other. On several occasions I had caught both of them exchanging hazel-eyed glances and also noticed the slight alteration in Kamini's tone when she spoke about him. But it was only after the first few months of their relationship that she had made me - her closest confidante - privy to her romantic liaison. Though a tinge disappointed, I wasn't completely oblivious to her inhibitions.

Nurturing a romantic relationship in a small town is very different from the way it works in larger cities. Couples live under the constant fear of being discovered and reprimanded by their parents. Dates, for the fright of being spotted by some or the other nosey relative are rare and usually it is only the most closely guarded of affiliations that manage to survive the test of time. Kamini was only being cautious.

Nirav's entry brought about a flurry of excitement in our otherwise mundane lives. We would draft mushy love letters for him, she would show me his text messages and we would compose and recompose appropriate replies, we would plot and scheme to enable them to meet and we would spend hours chatting about him – how he looked, how he behaved, how he spoke and dissecting every other sphere of his personality. Nirav was Kamini's boyfriend, but for the amount of my mind space he occupied, he might as well have been mine.

Our state of euphoria, however, was short lived and midway through the final year of college Nirav announced that his family was moving to Mumbai. His father had managed a transfer to the head office of the company he was employed with and was to shift base immediately. Nirav, along with the other family members, was to join him right after our final examinations.

Kamini was heartbroken and it took some effort on my part to ensure that her sanity was not compromised. Nirav too was extremely supportive and through numerous text messages and late night calls he attempted to subdue the pangs of separation for her. Eventually she came to terms with the cruel twist of fate and their cross border relationship continued with the blessings of telecom service providers, the World Wide Web and occasionally, the postal department.

For me, with his departure to Mumbai, Nirav had made a smooth exit from my life as well. It was only when Kamini told me about his plans to travel to Rajkot that old memories once again started streaming in front of my eyes. 'He is coming on the last day of

Navratri with a few friends from Mumbai. I will be seeing him after almost three years. Imagine!' she had literally lifted me off my feet and swirled around in circles till I felt my guts forming lumps in my throat.

We spent another half an hour in my room applying touches of make-up, helping each other pick the right match of accessories and admiring what the dressing table mirror reflected back at us. Kamini's anxiety had long settled beneath the desire to accentuate her appearance and I literally had to snatch my makeup kit from her before she grudgingly agreed to leave. A little after seven we mounted her Scooty and headed towards the Race Course ground. I knew that Kamini would have butterflies fluttering in her stomach, but strangely some of them seemed to have crept inside my tummy too.

'Wow, you girls are looking ravishing. You have been saving the best for the last… eh? I hope they have enough ambulances on standby today,' Deepali said, strolling up to us as within seconds of Kamini parking her Scooty in the earmarked parking area. As on the other days, we were to assemble near the entrance of the grand enclosure that had been erected for the celebrations.

Some of our friends were already there and others too were dribbling in at a rapid pace. In no time the group was large enough to qualify for a small military battalion – friends, friends of friends, cousins, distant relatives or anyone who knew someone from those already assembled continued to join us, exchanging introductions and pleasantries as they merged themselves with the rest.

Just then someone suggested that we enter the arena since most of the regular members of the group had already arrived. I glanced towards Kamini. Oblivious to the world around, she was intently staring at the road leading up to ground, an eager anticipation visible in her demeanor. Suddenly a glint appeared in her eyes and her lips stretched into a broad smile. I turned around and panned my vision to catch the object of her interest.

There he was! Nirav was casually strolling towards us, flanked by two other boys, perhaps his friends from the city. The trio was dressed in simple denims and tees, a striking contrast to the colorful dazzle of the festivities that surrounded us. After exchanging a fleeting smile with Kamini, subdued by the consciousness from the many faces that had now turned towards them, he waved in my direction. I waved back and took a few steps towards him.

'Hey, hey… Long time Buddy! How have you been?' Rajesh, one of the guys from our group overtook me and was now hugging Nirav. We Gujarati's are known to be an expressive lot and it was only after ample shaking and twisting that he eventually let go of him. Even before his feet could once again claim the burden of his weight, other members from the gang who knew Nirav from college pounced upon him.

Some of them, like Rajesh, probably knew that he was coming while the others looked pleasantly surprised with his sudden appearance. None though were aware of the real reason for his arrival, the reason that had stealthily walked up to my side and was now clinging on to my arm, making an effort to contain her excitement.

'This is Jacob… and he is Abhimanyu. Both of them work in the television industry in Mumbai. They were keen on witnessing the Dandiya celebrations here, so I brought them along,' Nirav introduced his friends to the group once the initial frenzy had settled. Like a sloppy caterpillar, the group then started steering itself towards the entrance and trickling into the arena. Kamini was maintaining a safe distance from Nirav and as far as I had noticed, they had refrained from exchanging even the most basic of pleasantries.

The large ground was illuminated with hundreds of halogen lamps and speakers mounted at regular intervals were discharging a familiar rhythmic beat. Groups of vibrantly dressed boys, girls, men, women and children were dancing about in circles, the synchronized collision of their Dandiya sticks adding a sense of vitality to the blaring music.

'Simply amazing Man! How different this is from the celebrations in Mumbai, the grandeur, the frenzy, the dazzle, it is all fantastic. Look, how coordinated they all are. Does the whole city keep practicing their dance moves all the year round?' Jacob, who was clearly awestruck with the scale and magnitude of celebrations, spoke to no one in particular. Let alone Gujarati, he couldn't converse even in Hindi and his English too had a peculiar but amusing accent to it. The word, 'Man' seemed his personalized punctuation and he said it with an additional emphasis on the 'a', making it sound more like 'Men'. His expressions too were exaggeratedly animated – dancing brows, eyes eager to pop out of their sockets and hands gesticulating at every possible opportunity.

Interesting fellow, I thought to myself as I went about playing an ideal host, explaining what the Navratri festivities meant for the habitants of Gujarat. 'You are right, the preparations begin much in advance. There are special dance classes to train people in Garba and Dandiya and people from all castes, classes and communities participate in the celebrations with equal fervor.' He listened to me intently, the feigned attention making him look even more comical. Despite my best efforts I could not contain a giggle.

'What Man! Why are you laughing now?' he retorted with a frown and I burst out into a full-fledged giddy laughter.

A band had now surfaced on the wooden stage towards one end of the ground and they were doling out devotional numbers to popular Bollywood tunes. Our guests found this extremely hilarious and soon they were dancing with the rest of us, clashing their imaginary sticks and swiveling with the awkwardness of a novice. Jacob in particular was putting a hilarious mix of Hip Hop and Dandia on display, moving with strange arm movements and pouted lips. I couldn't remember the last time I had laughed so much.

The frolic continued for hours with all of us dancing, cracking jokes, laughing and teasing each other. I noticed Kamini and Nirav exchange some cryptic glances, but they maintained their distance and hardly even spoke with each other. But the highlight of the evening clearly was Jacob. Both Abhimanyu and he had already earned themselves an elevated pedestal due to their intriguing line of work and Jacob, with his peculiarity and affability had easily become the center of attention for the entire group.

Later, at about midnight, when the celebrations concluded, we bid each other farewell with heavy hearts and headed towards our respective vehicles. As Kamini's Scooty, duly mounted by both of us, zipped past the rest of the group, I once again realized that she had not even exchanged any parting words with Nirav. Strange, I thought as we took the turn from the Race Course circle towards Raiya Road.

'Hey… hey… Where are you going? We need to go straight,' I bellowed, as Kamini steadied the vehicle post the sudden left-turn she had taken. 'We are going to Nirav's place,' she informed me matter-of-factly.

'What! Are you out of your mind?' I exclaimed. 'At this hour? You intend to get yourself killed or something… and me too, for no good reason?'

'Relax! His parents haven't come with him. It is just him and his two friends in the house and at this hour no one is going to see us getting in. We will leave from there before the break of dawn,' she reasoned.

'And what about our folks? What are we going to tell them?

'We can tell them that all the girls decided to stay back at Deepali's place. We have done that before, haven't we? Plus if both of us are together, they wont have reasons to suspect anything otherwise,' she argued.

Well, it wasn't as though I had never lied to my folks in the past, but spending an entire night with a bunch of boys seemed like an unreasonable stretch. On the other hand, I could feel a sudden surge of excitement brewing within me with the thought of meeting Jacob once again.

'You know that I haven't met him in three years. Tomorrow they are off to Gir and from there they will be returning to Mumbai. Tonight is all the time that I have with Nirav. Come on now, don't be such a spoil sport,' she almost pleaded. I don't know whether it was her pleading or the excitement within me which did the trick, but with a slight hum I was now a consenting party to the crime.

Kamini parked the Scooty between the gate of the house and a tree, concealing its presence from any prying neighbors. We tiptoed through the small lawn to the main door and Kamini tugged on it gently. It opened with a mild squeak. So, it wasn't a mere whim but a carefully hatched plan that had us sneaking into Nirav's house at such an insane hour. The familiarity with which Kamini was guiding me even cast a doubt on whether this was indeed the first time that she was visiting this place. 'Lovers and their secrets,' I shrugged.

As soon as we emerged from the dark passage into the drawing room, Nirav walked up and embraced Kamini. Not wanting to stand in the way of two aching hearts, I proceeded towards the sofa where Abhimanyu and Jacob were lounging. 'Hi beautiful, so we meet again,' Jacob welcomed me, as once again I shook hands with the duo. I responded with a smile.

'Thanks Sejal. Thanks for coming,' Nirav finally acknowledged my presence after escorting Kamini to the seating area. 'What can I make for you? Actually, we are slightly short of options, so will Vodka-Sprite do?' he asked.

'No no, I don't... I won't have anything,' I replied.

In my twenty three years I had never tasted alcohol and so, 'I don't drink,' would have been a more appropriate statement, yet in the last split-second I had switched the words to alter the sentence construction. Maybe 'I won't have' sounded better than 'I don't drink' – something to do with being in control and declining the offer rather than doing so because of my inability to take it on, I guess. I didn't want to be looked down upon by the city bred company we had, especially Jacob.

Despite the prohibition, booze wasn't a particularly scarce commodity in Rajkot. A phone call was all it took for the bottle of your choice to be delivered to right where you wanted it. Most of the house parties we were invited to, especially during Navratri when the moral fabric of the city was at its skimpiest best, had ample of the liquid flowing freely.

So, while the men ventured in and out of inebriation at will, the only visible impact of prohibition was that it had made drinking an even bigger taboo for us women folk. All it took was a glass in hand and a girl stood to be questioned on everything from her ethics and morality to her chastity and upbringing. Though this hadn't deterred most of the other girls from clandestinely tasting the prohibited liquid on some occasion or the other, I had somehow managed to hold on.

'Oh, so you don't drink?' Jacob seemed to have read through my carefully worded retort. I don't know whether the others noticed, but the underlying challenge in his tone was too stark to ignore. I glanced towards Nirav who was now pouring a drink for Kamini.

'Maybe I will have a small one too,' I said to him before looking back at Jacob. He was smiling.

I had an uneasy feeling as I held my first ever drink in my hand, but it was only momentary and started to settle with every sip I saw Kamini take from her glass. She was normal. She wasn't behaving like the drunkards I had seen in the movies. So maybe I would be able to endure it too. Just then I noticed Jacob's gaze on my glass and as a reaction I hurriedly lifted it up to my lips. The drink had a mildly pungent smell and a bitter aftertaste which remained once the sweetness of the mixer had worn off. It wasn't anything great but it wasn't too bad either.

After the first drink, Kamini and Nirav retired to one of the rooms to 'catch up' on the time they had lost. Soon after, Abhimanyu too complained of exhaustion and excused himself, leaving behind Jacob, me and an awkward silence.

'Must be strange, living in a city with no pubs or discotheques? You must come down to Mumbai sometime, there are hundreds of such joints and yet on weekends one has to stand in queues to gain entry into any of the decent ones,' Jacob broke the silence. I mumbled some incoherent words. The drink was having its effect, but contrary to my fears I was feeling nice – nice, happy and carefree.

He continued talking – telling me about his life in the city, the must-see places, the people – girls particularly, anecdotes from the world of television and movies and his work as an Assistant Director. 'You wouldn't recognize her if you see her in person. It is the lights, make-up and editing that makes her look the way she does on screen…' he was talking about some popular artist and I was staring blankly at him, admiring his husky voice, his sharp features, robust jaw-line, not realizing when I had shifted next to him on the sofa and rested my head on his shoulder.

He was now stroking my hair with his fingers, it felt nice. Then suddenly I felt his face close to mine. So close that his stubble was brushing against my cheeks. And then it happened. My first real kiss! Some of you might think that at twenty three it was high time it happened, if it ever was to, but you would be surprised at the number of girls in Rajkot who remain deprived of even a male touch right up till their wedding night.

We remained entangled on the sofa for as long as I could remember. His hands hungrily exploring parts of my body that no one had touched thus far, his well-sculpted chest beating against my own and our lips locked into each other – nibbling, sucking and exploring. On a couple of occasions I remember him trying to untie my Ghaghara, but something within me made him stop. Even in my inebriated and excited state, I was conscious about my boundaries and he understandingly obliged by ceasing his efforts to breach them.

It was with the sound of someone clearing his throat that we hurriedly moved away from each other and frantically started to straighten our disheveled clothes. After a minute or two Nirav emerged from the bedroom and close on his heels was Kamini. She had a satisfied smile on her face as she signaled towards me, shifting my attention towards the wall-clock. It was four a.m. already and if we were to enter our respective houses without being spotted, we had to make a move now.

Kamini hugged Nirav and planted a parting kiss on his lips – a surprisingly brazen and audacious display of affection for the girl I knew. I stuck to the traditional handshake for my farewells and we were once again scaling the streets of Rajkot on the Scooty.

'So, what are your plans? Nirav and you, I mean,' I asked for the want of anything else to discuss. I hadn't slept all night and I had serious doubts on whether Kamini had too. The last thing I wanted was for one of us to doze off on the Scooty.

'I will be moving to Mumbai. I have been looking for a job there and something should get finalized in a week or two. I will work there for a couple of years and then we will get married,' she replied in a serious tone, steering the vehicle to avoid a pothole on the road.

'Oh… and your parents, have they agreed?'

'I haven't spoken with anyone yet. I will tell them once my job is finalized,' she replied. I knew that the 'anyone' included me and she was justifying not having shared her plans with me earlier, but I was too preoccupied with my thoughts to fret over such petty issues.

Later that day and for some days to follow, I kept struggling with a plethora of emotions. Guilt, at having done what I did – making out with a guy I barely knew. Hell, I didn't even know if he had a girlfriend or… or, whether he was married even. Isn't this what they call a one-night-stand? How could I behave in such a slutty fashion?

My parents, this is what I give them in return for their blind faith and trust?

For days together I could barely look my parents in the eye. I tried to keep myself occupied with studies, household chores or anything else that gave me an excuse to not face them. I spent hours in the seclusion of the bathroom, trying in vain to scrub the guilt off my body. I prayed to the Gods for forgiveness and I resolved to not repeat such a mistake ever again.

Then there were the butterflies in my stomach and the confusion within my mind - Jacob's rugged looks, his sense of humor and his charming personality. Was he too thinking about me the way I was thinking about him? Was it just a surge of hormones for him or did we strike a chord at some deeper level? Do I love him? Does he love me? No, how can I possibly love him when I barely know him? Then, what exactly was it that had transpired? Why do I keep thinking about him?

The experience too replayed itself in my head, not as often as the other thoughts, but I did relive it every once in a while – usually when I was alone on my bed. His touch, his fingers, his lips, his chest, the warmth of his body, the urgency of his movements, all of them would come back to me in a surging flash. When this happened, it brought about a strong desire, almost a need, for me to fondle and play with myself. It was only after I had given in to my urges that the feeling passed as suddenly as it had appeared.

I did not discuss Jacob and what happened between us with anyone, not even Kamini. There were times when I yearned to call him, to hear his voice, but I had been foolish enough not to ask him for his number and now it would be odd for me to ask Kamini to ask Nirav for his number. And he was the man, so wasn't he the one who was supposed to call?

A week, a fortnight and even a month went by, but Jacob did not call. I refrained from bring up his name in front of Kamini for the fear of the discussion steering towards what I now considered to be my deep dark secret. Jacob was still there in my mind, but the intensity of my memories was diminishing. I was slowly coming to terms with the fact that the happenings of that night weren't exactly my first brush with love but actions guided by lust and mere physical attraction. It made me feel cheap and degraded but it was still better than losing my sleep over a fairytale that never was and would never be.

I had tried shifting a part of the blame to the drinks, Kamini, Navratri and anything else I could think of, but the pain refused to subside. It was only when I accepted to myself my own role in the happenings, conscious or otherwise, that the burden eventually lifted. 'Ok, he had his share of fun… the Bastard! But what the heck, I enjoyed myself too,' I constantly told myself, not providing any fodder of sympathy and self-pity to my bruised and victimized side.

It was soon after that Kamini broke the news. She had found a job with a call center, one that was paying enough for her to sustain herself in Mumbai, and in less than a month she would be leaving Rajkot to pursue her dreams.

I should have felt sad since my best friend was soon to relocate to a different city, but I was happy. I was happy for her and I was happy because the cloud of uncertainty from my own life too seemed to be lifting. Suddenly I knew what I wanted to do. I too would be shifting to Mumbai. If not for Jacob - the asshole who had not bothered to call me even once - at least for the world and the life I had witnessed briefly through his words and his eyes.

THREE

It was a little before nine that we reached the Limbda Chowk bus stand from where I was to board a bus that would take me a step closer to my dreams. Despite my meek protests my father had insisted on accompanying me and I didn't quite mind. His presence did allay the cramps of anxiety that were entangling my intestines, but I was too insolent to acknowledge that, even to my own self.

I did not know what exactly my dreams were or even the expectations I had from my destination, the big-bad city of Mumbai. But there was an optimistic energy and a nervous enthusiasm about stepping out into the unknown, unshielded and completely on my own.

'Remember, you are going there because you want to. But if things don't turn out the way you would like them to, board the very next bus and return home. We are all there for you, always! Take care of yourself and may Lord Balaji remove all obstacles from your path,' my father said, handing me a packet of potato wafers and a bottle of water.

I could see right through his façade of bravado and relate to the pain and anguish he was bottling up within. It obviously wasn't easy for him to send off his loved, pampered and only daughter into the crevice of uncertainty. I was suddenly glad that my mother had decided to stay back home as I hugged him for one last time and walked towards my designated seat in the Volvo bus.

'Seju, take good care of yourself beta,' were the last words I heard from him as, with a roar, the bus eased out of the station. On my next seat was an elderly gentleman who had by now buried his nose within the pages of the thick novel he was clutching. I was glad. I wasn't particularly in the mood for frivolous chit-chat and breeding unwarranted familiarity with my co-passengers. Reclining my seat a little further, I shut my eyes and permitted my thoughts to wander about unchecked.

Four months had passed since Kamini's departure from Rajkot. Along with her parents, I too had come to the bus stand to see her off. I had felt a similar surge of excitement back then, watching the bus ferry her towards her destiny as I waved to her from the pavement. I wondered whether it had been the same bus that I was sitting in and I contemplated on whether Kamini too would have been there to bid me farewell had I been the pioneer in embarking upon this journey. My thoughts were making full use of the liberties I had graced them with.

Initially I had refrained from sharing with her the idea of following her to Mumbai that was sprouting within my head. Instead I had given myself to tracking Kamini's progress in the city and the information I thus gathered, I was conveniently using to firm up my own plans.

She had initially lodged herself with some distant relatives and within a week found a flat for herself, with Nirav's help of course. 'It is a small one room set, much smaller than our rooms back in Rajkot, but it is nice – not too far from office and a ten minute walk from where Nirav stays,' she had informed me.

She would call me a couple of times during the week and share in brief her experiences at work, at home or of the city in general. It was only when I called her that she would get into details, sometimes stretching our conversations even to a couple of hours. Once again I understood her predicament; some financial machinations were warranted when you were fending for yourself in a big city without the comfort of home and the soothing presence of parents. So I had taken to disconnecting her calls on some or the other pretext and calling her back a little later to save talk-time on her mobile connection. After all my bills were still paid by my father. But for how long now, I would find myself wondering?

'This place that Nirav took me to... An open air lounge bar right next to the sea, I could spend my entire life just sitting there and staring into the unending pool of water. Jacob and his girlfriend were also there. You remember Jacob, don't you?' I wondered whether she was still ignorant of the brief escapade that Jacob and I had embarked upon during his visit to Rajkot. As she went about describing how she felt that Jacob had been shortchanged and deserved someone significantly better than the 'whorish bitch' he was dating, I couldn't help a smile from surfacing on my face. The Bastard! Each one gets just what he deserves.

Every time I spoke with her my curiosity about life in the big city and my resolve to get there at the earliest only strengthened. I prepared my resume and uploaded it on various job portals, looking to emulate the steps that Kamini had taken for her liberation. I had started day-dreaming about Mumbai, its people, its culture, and Rajkot with its lackadaisical existence had started becoming somewhat of an irritant. I had started hating the lazy air that seemed to be perennially enveloping everything and everyone around. I no longer liked the Gathias, Fafdas and Undhiyo that I had savored all along and even the language, the inelegant mix of Hindi, Gujarati and Kathiawadi that people spoke, was becoming a source of constant annoyance.

My frustrations were further mounting since none of the countless companies I had applied for jobs in had found my candidature worthy of even a measly revert. An occasional placement consultant did bother to call, but my current location was quick to dilute any interest that my profile might have generated. It was obviously much easier for them to summon someone who was in the same city for an interview in comparison with an outstation candidate and neither my qualifications and nor my non-existent work experience made me a highly revered commodity for potential employers.

'I am coming to Mumbai,' I blurted out to Kamini in a fit of frustration. 'When? For how many days? Uncle and aunty are also coming or are you coming alone? Where will you be putting up?' she ambushed me with a flurry of questions in turn.

'No, I mean… I am also planning to shift to Mumbai. Get myself a job and stay there... Like you!' I responded sheepishly.

'Oh, ok!' her excitement had visibly waned, possibly because the idea might have come across as far-fetched and distant. 'And, have you found yourself a job?' she shot back with her next question.

'No, not as yet, but I have made my resume and started circulating it,' I replied.

'So why don't you mail it to me as well? I will share it with the hiring manager in my company and also check with Nirav if there is something that he can refer you for. Is there anything specific you have in mind?'

'No, nothing in particular. Any nice job with a nice company would do.' Reaching Mumbai had been my primary agenda and I had not risen from it to ponder over the type of job I wanted. Moreover my initial brush with job hunt had taught me better than to erect any barriers of expectations. 'I will send you my CV tomorrow itself,' I added.

Kamini shared my profile within her company and Nirav apparently shared it within his circle of friends and acquaintances, but time kept running and nothing worth a mention materialized from anywhere. 'It takes time; but when you do get an interview call, everything will happen in a jiffy. Imagine the amount of fun we will have once you are here. I can't wait for things to materialize for you.' Kamini tried all tricks in the book to prevent my motivation from dipping, but patience had never been one of my notable virtues.

Just when doubts on the workability of the entire scheme had started creeping in, I received a call from a placement consultant. It was an ad sales profile with a smalltime outdoor media company. They owned several billboards, signage sites, television screens in shopping malls and commercial complexes and various other properties that could be rented by advertisers to promote their products. The job was to find parties willing to spend a bit to advertise their products, simple.

The job seemed perfectly cut out for me, I was excited. How difficult could it be to find people who were looking to advertise their products or services in a city like Mumbai? With the plethora of companies, industries, retail chains and not to forget, the film industry, I would probably run a risk of being hounded by potential customers.

'Oh, you are not based in Mumbai, is it?' the concern that had crept into the caller's voice on coming to know of my coordinates brought my soaring ambitions crashing down in no time. 'I am not in Mumbai, but I can travel anytime you want me to. I need the job, please…,' I found myself nearly pleading.

'But the company will not be reimbursing your expenses. Is that fine?'

'Yes, that works for me,' I eagerly responded.

'Ok, let me forward your profile to them and let's see what they think of it.' Thanking the stranger who had appeared like a solitary ray of hope amidst all the moroseness, I disconnected the call.

Convincing my parents, the next hurdle ahead of me, was not as easy as I had anticipated. They, especially my concerned mother, were fretful about everything in Mumbai from the high-rises, traffic, boys, food, water, sea, and trains to the political party that had been hitting headlines for their anti-migrant stance and antics. With Kamini already in Mumbai, I had a valid counter for each of their apprehensions – if she can do it, so can I - despite which it took me almost a week before they agreed to allow me to attend the interview. The condition was that my father would escort me to Mumbai and back.

Kamini had been right. When it does happen, it happens in a flash without permitting time for even a blink. Within a few days the consultant called back with the details of my interview which was scheduled a week later and thus happened my first real brush with Mumbai. It was a morning-evening affair; we took the overnight bus to the city and booked ourselves for return the same evening.

The interview, my first attempt at seeking employment, was scheduled for 11.00 a.m. and after a quick stop at a nearby restaurant for breakfast and freshening up, we headed straight to the venue. The interaction, like the office, wasn't anything grand and it did not even come close to justifying the edginess I was experiencing before stepping into the room.

A solitary interviewer, a man whose name I forgot within moments of his introduction, asked me a bunch of simple questions spanning across my academic and personal background before handing me a pen and asking me to sell it to him. It was a cheap ball-point pen, like the ones you find being sold on bus stands and railway stations, but I was up to the task.

I offered him one pen free if he bought two, blurted out some imaginary advantages that this particular make of pens had over its more expensive counterparts and gave him a logical reason to procure three pens instead of one. 'Gift it to the children in the house. It is a much better thing to give than chocolates, which are bad for their teeth.' He smiled and informed me that my interview was over and I could expect to hear from them soon.

'How did it go?' was all that my father enquired. Obviously, he wasn't particularly keen about my interview or about the job per say. In fact, for all I know, he could well have been praying for me to fare badly, like I was sure my mother would have been.

I had informed Kamini of our visit and since she had a night shift at work, she had insisted that we meet up for lunch. The venue was another nondescript restaurant, one that she had recommended, and I was glad to meet my friend after the gap of many months. She had changed, she looked different, sleeker, tidier, prettier and with an air of maturity in her appearance and conduct.

'Wow, wouldn't it be amazing if you got the job? You can move in with me, I wouldn't even have to look for a roommate then,' she said, after I had given her a complete download of the interview. She then looked towards my father and spotting his gloom, added, 'Don't worry uncle. Mumbai is very different from Rajkot, but it is a very safe city. She will learn a lot about life by staying here, plus I am there to take care of her.'

My father voiced his appreciation for her comforting words but I could see that he wasn't completely convinced just as yet. 'One step at a time. Let the interview results come out first,' I told myself, as I shifted my attention back towards Kamini. I quizzed her about her life, work, the city, things that we had discussed telephonically on umpteen occasions, but I couldn't keep from enquiring about in person. There were various other questions brewing within me, but my father's hawk-like presence prohibited me from dwelling upon them. Eventually, we bid her a goodbye and hailed an auto for the Borivali depot to board the bus back to Rajkot.

My first encounter with the city had only been a cameo, too small for me to pronounce any judgments, but it had managed to arouse enough curiosity for me to remain lost in daydreams upon my return. I now had several images in my mind, which when paired with my thoughts transformed the city into a fantasy land. However this state of trance was fairly short-lived, as within a few days the consultant called once again, this time to apprise me of my selection. The compensation offered was meager, but hell, for a life in Mumbai I was prepared to make do even with peanuts.

I was thrilled and overjoyed. Contrastingly though, the atmosphere within my house took up a deathly, morose appearance as soon as the news percolated. Not much was spoken or discussed. My parents had shifted their dependency to the echoes of silence for expressing their dissent and I decided against interfering. The decision had been made when they had reluctantly permitted me to attend the interview and now that the results had turned out favorable, I was in no mood to go through the rites all over again.

The preparations for my departure were undertaken mechanically, a grumpy silence clouding all pertinent actions. I was taken out to shop for clothes, a new cell phone, and items of domestic utility; given instructions on what not to do, enough to fill up an entire manual and too complex to be attributed much space in my mind; and I was laden with enough home-made snacks to possibly feed all the hungry souls in the city for days together. But for me all that mattered was that the day that I had toiled for had eventually arrived. The bus after a couple of brief halts – one for dinner at a highway Dhaba and another to pick up some passengers from the outskirts of Ahmedabad, was speeding away, tearing through the dark roads, towards its destination.

FOUR

The bus dropped me at Andheri on the Western Express Highway and following Kamini's instructions, I headed towards one of the waiting autos. Mumbai looked pristine in the early hours of the morning sans the crawling traffic and bustling sea of humanity. A mildly pungent smell, like that of a carpet in desperate need for some sunlight, was sailing through the air, but it wasn't disconcerting to the least. For me, it was a flavor of the life that I had carved for myself and I was looking forward to living every day of it.

I was still admiring the city – its vertical expanse, the maze of roads and flyovers - when a sudden jarring noise startled me off my wits. 'Dhoom machale, dhoom macha le,' with some play of switches near the handle, the auto driver had brought his stereo to life which was now screaming the title track of a recent Bollywood blockbuster right into my ears.

'Bhaia,' annoyed, I called out aloud, only to be greeted by a display of strained and decaying teeth. 'Angrezi gane nahi hain madam (I don't have English songs),' he replied sheepishly. 'That's ok. Just reduce the volume before I lose my eardrums,' I said.

In just under half an hour I was outside Kamini's door, pressing the door bell. After subjecting my fingers to a reasonable bit of exercise, the door finally opened and a sleepy head popped out. 'Seju!' she screamed, her sleep evaporating, as we hugged each other laughing uncontrollably as though we were meeting after a lifetime.

The flat comprised of a bedroom and a small hall cum kitchen cum dining room cum study cum whatever else one desired for it to be. The entire structure was barely a few feet larger than my own room back in Rajkot, but it seemed to accommodate much more than it was perhaps intended to originally.

On one end of the hall was a slab which, with the single-burner stove, some utensils and the adjoining sink, betrayed its utility as the kitchen. The other side, separated by the unmarked passage leading to the bedroom, comprised of a television mounted over a wooden trolley. Facing it were two comfortable looking cane chairs and a small settee. A bright purple wall, in sharp contrast to the other pale-pink ones, was adorned with neatly framed posters of old Hindi movies.

'Here! I have emptied this side for you,' Kamini said, dragging my bag to the cupboard cum wardrobe in the bedroom. She had emptied one half of it for me to keep my things. I couldn't help but glance towards the other half which was still occupied; her wardrobe too seemed to have undergone a transformation. The bedroom had a small window, a queen-size bed, our shared cupboard and a music system which was connected by dangling wires to the two large speakers hanging from two corners of the ceiling.

'I love the place,' I mumbled, walking towards the window, half expecting to catch a glimpse of the sea but to be greeted instead by thatched roofs of a slum dwelling. May be I had spoken too soon. And thank god that we were on the seventh floor, for I was certain that the view I saw was bound to be accompanied by a smell that would have made a task out of even the basic act of breathing for us.

'It could have been better, but at 12,000 rupees this was the best I could manage,' Kamini replied. 'What! You are paying… so much for just this?' I exclaimed. One could have rented an entire bungalow for that kind of money in Rajkot. Ok, I am exaggerating, but still! 'Welcome to Mumbai,' she replied with a knowing smirk.

I had given myself a couple of days to settle down before I was to join work and in those couple of days we chatted and gossiped, went shopping, cooked, talked a little more, lazed around and did everything that our hearts' willed. Kamini too had managed to schedule her two weekly offs to coincide with my arrival and we allowed ourselves to drift, like carefree birds soaring in the skies, and soak in every precious moment that went by.

'How about Nirav, how is he doing?' I checked with her. Of course I wanted to know about Jacob too, but purely out of curiosity and nothing else. 'I am sure he is fine,' popped a nonchalant reply.

'Why, you guys have had a tiff or something?'

'Not exactly. Just that, things didn't seem to be working out between us anymore. Anyways, that is history now so let us focus on what lies ahead instead. How about you, all set to join office tomorrow?' She had deftly evaded the question and inquisitive as I was, I knew Kamini better than to pursue the topic any further. She would tell me about it when she felt like and there was no way she was revealing anything prior to that.

A couple of weeks at work and I had transformed into a living paradox – a thoroughly screwed-up virgin. I couldn't even begin to imagine how off the mark I had been from the reality of my job in the convenience of my thoughts. Selling a two Rupee pen in a deliberated role play was one thing and selling millions worth of hoarding and bus-shelter spaces to often unwilling buyers was completely another.

After a brief training I was assigned to a team of five that was responsible for generating business from the Pharmaceutical and Financial Services sectors. The entire sales team was divided into two verticals. While the first one focused on managing relationships with media buying companies and was responsible for majority of the company's business, the vertical to which I belonged focused on Direct Sales to customers.

My vertical was further divided into six teams that were responsible for extracting business from clients in specific sectors which were allocated to them for the sake of focus and to avoid internal conflicts. The Direct Sales Vertical, as it was referred to, was headed by Promila Khanna, a thick-set lady in her late thirties who was devoid of any lady-like mannerisms. If there was anyone I thought to be in a desperate need for a heart transplant, it was her.

She held weekly review meetings with all the teams and any team that seemed likely to fall short of its target was inevitably exposed to her brutal ire. She did not hesitate in involving friends, family and sometimes even the ancestors of the guilty parties, often showering them with expletives that were as acidic as vinegar.

In the first review meeting I attended, though not directly in the line of fire, I was left trembling from the knees below. During my first week on the job itself I knew that if I was to ever miss my monthly target, it would either leave me dead because of suicide or behind bars on charges of murder.

Our five member team was headed by Ravi, a friendly and sensible fellow who was barely a few years older than I was. The rest of us were paired up into two for approaching potential clients. I was paired with Rajneesh Chatterjee (Chatu, as he was more popularly known around office) a barely twenty adolescent whose interests panned across everything other than the one he was being paid for. He claimed to have completed his graduation from Kolkata, a feat that his appearance and conduct belied, and was in Mumbai for the past one year looking for a suitable acting break. If he was to be believed, he could sing, dance, choreograph and even handle the camera. 'This is only for the interim – a stopgap thingy. Wait till I get my first big break,' he often mused.

We were handed a bunch of printouts with names and addresses of companies from our allocated sectors by Ravi as he doled out our target for the month. 'Twenty lacks worth of billing,' he had blurted without a twitch. The figure didn't mean anything to me. It could have been two million or twenty, for all I cared. I was yet to familiarize myself with the nuances of the business and I had to depend on Chatu, a man who hardly looked dependable, to help me sail through my first month.

Spotting my predicament Ravi added, 'Don't worry, Rajneesh knows the job well. He has been with us for six months now and already has a reasonable pipeline of clients. The only thing you need to ensure is that he keeps his head down and focuses on work and not his extracurricular engagements.' Hardly reassured, I nodded in acknowledgement as Chatu continued to wear his it-don't-bother-me smirk.

Thus began my grind and the tussle to survive without facing one of Promila's dreaded onslaughts. A quick look around was enough to cipher that I wasn't exactly placed on the most comfortable of footings. While half the outdoor properties were busy promoting new tele-soaps and to-be-released films, the other half were unequally distributed between builders wanting to sell flats, garment retailers advertising their wares and telecom companies striving to outdo each other. In an age when every second person needs a loan or a credit card and new-age diseases are creeping up like monsoon mushrooms, why would Banks and Pharma companies spend their millions in putting up hoardings to woo customers?

My immediate concern though was to get Chatu to work. When he was not on a flight of fantasy, sharing near-visual details of his imminent success as an actor, he would simply vanish at the slightest pretext. And sometimes even the pretext was duly omitted. 'I am not feeling well, had a late night session with a script writer yesterday.

Why don't you carry on with the first couple of meetings, just keep noting what the clients say and I will catch up with you a little later,' he would dish out a story as soon as we emerged from the office, duly armed with a call-plan of meeting four different clients during the day.

The second weekly review for the month was due and I had only managed about six joint calls with Chatu and another eight customers that I had met on my own. Most customers had simply turned us away, while a few had promised to call us back when they were planning to launch an advertising campaign. Net-net, the only one lead that could be termed as warm, and only just, was the proprietor of a small-time Pharma company that I had met. The company was engaged in sourcing OTC (over the counter) medicines and marketing them under their own brand.

As usual, Chatu had had been missing that day too. He had to tend to an ailing aunt or something, and that when barely a few days back he had told me that he had no relatives in the city. Simply incorrigible he was. We had spoken to this guy a couple of days back when he had agreed to meet us today. Not wanting to let the opportunity slide away, I decided to make a solo appearance instead of waiting for my partner's non-existent relative to recover.

The burly man was seated on a throne-like leather chair behind a large wooden desk. The walls of the small room were plastered with garish maroon velvet wallpaper on which numerous gold frames with images of deities were hanging. The air bore the distinct odor of cigarettes mixed with the flowery scent of a freshener which, no doubt, had been liberally used to make the enclosure breathable. A chill ran through me as I entered the office. No it wasn't fear, just that the air conditioner, set on an artic-like temperature, was making its presence felt. With the excessive layers of fat that covered the occupant, any warmer and perhaps the room would have become uninhabitable for him.

'Come Madame. Tell me... What can I do for you?' he spoke with the air of a seasoned businessman, as I shriveled my existence on the chair facing him. It was the first time that I had got such a willing listener for the sales pitch that I had relentlessly practiced and rehearsed. So I took off instantly lest something made him change his mind.

I kept talking for a good ten minutes, explaining various innovative communication mediums that we could offer and how they would help him grow his business and multiply his profits. He listened intently, his gaze not moving away from my face for even a fraction. 'So, what do you think Sir? Would you want to try out some of these options for promoting your brands?' I said, after I had finished running through the pitch uninterrupted.

'Sharma, Dilbagh Sharma... that is my name. I would like it if you addressed me by my name rather than 'Sir',' he said, flashing a 1000 watt smile. 'Fine Mr. Sharma,' I returned the smile. 'No... Not Mister, only Sharma! That's what my friends call me,' he exclaimed. 'Ha ha... Fine then, Sharma. It sounds a little odd though, addressing you by your surname,' I replied. I seemed to be making some headway with my pitch and I would have readily addressed him as Amitabh Bachchan, if he so desired.

'Yes, that is much better,' a visibly satisfied Sharma continued. 'You know how the market is these days. The big players have much deeper pockets and they are trying to gobble up small fries like us by aggressive pricing and campaigns. I was anyways planning to do something for one of our products – a pain relief balm brand - so, good that you came along. Oh, how stupid of me, what will you have? Tea, Coffee, Cold Drink?'

'No no, nothing. I am fine,' I was anyways feeling amply rejuvenated by the direction of the conversation flow. I could see Ravi's beaming face and the I-knew-you-have-it-in-you look in his eyes when I would break the news of having closed a deal. 'Aisa kaise (How can that be). You are our guest, so you must give us an opportunity to serve you something,' he said before picking up the telephone receiver and yelling into the mouthpiece. 'Do thandha behjna (Send in two cold drinks)'

'Sejal Patel, so you are a Gujarati?' he was now toying with the Business Card I had handed him at the very start of our meeting. I nodded. 'And how long have you been here, in Mumbai?'

'Not very long, its only been a few months that I shifted here,' I replied, without divulging much details, especially that I was only as old in the city as perhaps the stubble he was sporting. He went on to quiz me about my family, friends, what all I had seen of Mumbai yet and other such inconsequential stuff before stumbling upon the topic of interest; his, not mine. 'Why don't we catch up for coffee sometime… at the Lotus Café… J W Marriot hotel? We can get to know each other better and also discuss as to what is the best that you can offer,' he said, smearing me with a hungry glare from head to toe.

I was appalled. I knew that this loathsome barter of seeking favors of one kind against another was a way of life for some. I had also heard about girls who looked at such propositions as an opportunity to make a quick buck on the side. I wasn't being judgmental or questioning Sharma's brazen attempt to score at the first possible opportunity – if there was any chance for a man with his looks to get laid, it had to originate through such means – only I was poignant at finding myself at the receiving end of the overture.

'I will get back to you on that, in the meantime I have another meeting lined up, so I shall take your leave now,' I said, abruptly gathering my belongings and making an exit. I didn't look back to check Sharma's reaction but I was sure that his eyes would be following the sway of my bottom as I walked out. The bastard!

I had relegated the incident to some obscure corner of my memory, not mentioning it to Chatu or even to Kamini until today. Ravi had summoned all members of our team for a meeting to take stock of our achievements before the actual review with Promila happened. The other pair, Shibani and Purohit shared the details of a deal they were hoping to ink within the next couple of days. A verbal agreement had been reached with the client and only the formal documentation and signing was pending. After praising their efforts, Ravi shifted his focus towards us.

Chatu began muttering names of clients, some that we had met together and others whose names I had never heard earlier. His steady drone was soon interrupted by Ravi. 'Cut the crap and tell me about the business that you are expecting to close,' he barked. Chatu stuttered and stammered while I remained silent. We were both falling short of words and Ravi was boring into us with his eyes when suddenly a flash occurred. 'There is this one guy I had met. Initially he did seem interested in launching a customer campaign, but then...' I went on to narrate the entire experience with Sharma and his near indecent proposal that had made me walk away from his office. 'I don't know, but maybe we can try and convert him,' I added.

'Why didn't you tell me about this? A coffee was all that he invited you for, what was the god damned harm in accepting the invite? Every client who is paying through his nose needs some bit of ego massage. The guy obviously wouldn't have forced you to sleep with him,' bellowed a clearly agitated Chatu.

'Maybe if you were there in the meeting, he wouldn't have dared to make such an offer at all and maybe we would have closed the deal right there, sitting in his office. How on earth do you know that he wouldn't have forced himself upon me? You were not the one tolerating his lusty eyes checking every portion of your body,' I yelled back.

'Enough! Cut this out, both of you. Rajneesh, we are here to do business and not sell ourselves to clients. If he did make such an offer, she had every right to walk out from there. And about you not accompanying her for the call please see me after the review meeting and we shall discuss. Sejal, you please call Sharma once again and tell him that you would like to see him once more. Try and schedule the meeting in his office, else even a coffee shop would do. I will accompany you for the meeting; let's see what he's got. And yes, don't mention that you would not be coming alone,' Ravi intervened to bring the argument to its conclusion.

In the review meeting Ravi started by updating Promila about the deal that Shibani and Purohit were working on, showering her with minute details of the arrangement – number of properties that the client would be procuring, the negotiated rates and the resulting margins. And then dexterously, in a single sentence, he summed up the other positive leads that were to be pursued over the next few days, Sharma's name also featuring among them. He had managed to steer us clear of certain reprimand and as she shifted her focus to one of the other teams, I heaved a sigh of relief and thanked all the deities whose names I could recall.

Lately Kamini had been vociferous with her complaints about my excessive indulgence with work, and quite rightly so. 'These days are never going to come back dear! If you spend your entire day slogging out for your employers and the nights worrying about what the next day has in store, just when do you intend to live your own life? Take it light babes,' she would often counsel.

The uncertainties that came with Chatu as an associate had engulfed my entire existence. When I was not wandering about the city hoping to stumble across a willing client, I would be lost in my thoughts, dreading the upshot of my non-performance. By late evenings, when I usually returned home, Kamini was either already out or just about leaving for her shift at work.

She had also enrolled herself with a manpower agency and took up odd jobs as a promoter in exhibitions or events to 'make ends meet'. 'They pay pretty well, 2 to 3 thousand for half a days work and all you need to do is stand there smiling. Let me know if you are keen. I can put you on to them,' she had attempted to let me in on the scheme, but in vain. Sunday, the one weekly off I got from work was necessary for me to recuperate and finish other basic chores like laundry, a visit to the parlor etcetera and so I had no option but to let the offer pass. And since her new engagement kept her occupied on most Sundays, we hardly ever got time to talk and were virtually like two strangers sharing the same roof.

After the last review meeting life at work had marginally improved for me. I did not know what had transpired between Chatu and Ravi, but Chatu had barely spoken to me ever since. The very next day Ravi had accompanied me for my scheduled calls and since then we had become a regular working pair. In our team huddle before the next review I had learnt that Chatu had been put on a 'Performance Improvement Plan' and had been doled out a target for the next three months that he had to achieve single-handedly for the sake of retaining his job. The slight tinge of guilt I felt wasn't too difficult to brush aside. We were all employees of the company and it was only fair that we put in the efforts expected against the paychecks we received.

Sharma had turned out to be a hoax. He sounded pretty excited when I had called him and had readily agreed to meet me in his office the very next day. He was somewhat startled when I walked in with Ravi, introducing him as my boss who was there to close out the finer details of the campaign. Sharma had given some general spiel about wanting to defend his market-share against the onslaught by larger players but when Ravi started probing further on the specifics of his plan and the monetary outlay he had in mind, his replies started becoming vague and roundabout. Taking a cue from his words we cordially alighted, asking him to call us once his plan was ready.

'He is not the only one of his kind; you will find many such assholes in this line of work. It is important to figure out whether their interest is genuine or merely a farce to impress a pretty girl,' Ravi had summarized his take on the meeting. By 'pretty girl' he could have meant just about anyone, but strangely I felt somewhat flattered and allowed myself to blush a little.

Ravi had now started accompanying me for all my calls, deftly handling customer queries and providing clarifications when sought. The fact that he had worked his way up the ladder showed as he tactfully convinced them into experimenting with the media vehicles our company had to offer. With some customers he already shared a rapport, perhaps from his days in frontline sales, making it considerably easier for us to gain a patient audience. With each call we made, I found myself admiring his skills and intellect all the more.

In between calls we would halt for our lunch and coffee breaks and then he would adorn a completely different hat, behaving more like a friend than as a boss. He would enquire about my family back home, talk to me about his own, and generally discuss any other topic that caught his fancy. From cricket to the latest movie releases and from weather to politics, he seemed well informed about everything and I enjoyed simply sitting there and listening to him.

The zone of comfort his sheer presence propelled me into allowed me to share with him my innermost feelings and emotions, those that I had sometimes shielded even from my own self. He was my first friend in Mumbai, barring Kamini of course, and I was glad to have met him. He too seemed to enjoy my company as often after a tiring day in the field he would offer to drop me back and occasionally we would halt somewhere along the way for dinner as well.

He hailed from Nagpur and shared a rented flat in Powai with a couple of friends. My abode did not exactly fall on his route back home and so whenever he insisted on dropping me, I found myself basking in a heady, warm feeling. He was just about average in terms of looks, medium height, dark complexion and ordinary features, but as I sat behind him on his bike there were times that I felt like pressing myself against him, gripping him tightly and feeling the warmth of his body against mine. There were a few random instances when I had given in to my urges on the pretext of a pothole or a sharp turn, with adequate precautions to avoid exposing the premeditation behind them of course.

He was a nice guy and I enjoyed his company. In fact it won't be totally inaccurate to say that I longed to be with him, listen to him talk or to simply stare at him, sitting quietly. Was it love? Was one of the many fears my parents had voiced while allowing me to shift to Mumbai actually taking form? Well, whatever it was, as long as I was happy swimming in its tides, the need for a hasty retreat did not really arise.

FIVE

'I am not taking 'No' for an answer. Today we are going out partying and there is not going to be any further debate on it. Get ready, 15 minutes are all you have,' Kamini was clearly in no mood to relent. It was a Saturday and the next day was an off for me. Also, I had just finished my first month at work, and a successful one at that since Ravi and I had managed to close two deals and even the team as a whole had overachieved the targets. A celebration of some sort was certainly warranted.

'Ok.. Ok.. But will you at least tell me where we are going?'

'Yippee,' she screamed happily, planting a peck on my cheek. 'That's my girl! I am in the mood to party and get drunk today… We could go to this new place, Fusion, that has recently opened in Juhu?'

When it came to night-spots, I was hardly competent enough to have an opinion. The name Fusion sounded familiar, but after a slight thought I realized that I had seen the name on a signage outside a garment store in Rajkot – one that I crossed twice a day on my way to and from the university. 'Cool,' I said, heading towards the bedroom for a quick change.

'Is this what you intend to wear?' a gaping Kamini greeted me as I emerged from the room. I was wearing denims and a pink tank top – the most 'modern' pieces of clothing I had in my wardrobe. Alarmed, I looked at her and then at my own self. 'Yes. Why?'

'Don't be crazy. This is good for going to a mall but not for going to a night club. Here, try this,' she said, extracting a black dress from her side of the wardrobe. I had seen her wearing the dress earlier and knew that it did little to cover ones body. Its deep neckline was slightly disconcerting, and the soft fabric tugged on to the body betraying every little sway and twitch of the parts it did manage to conceal. As I hesitantly looked at her, she shot back, 'What now? Don't be crazy. All girls at the club will be decked up and you don't want to stand there feeling like a scarecrow, do you? Moreover, who are you worried about, it is only the two of us who are going. So don't waste time and wear it quickly.'

What the heck, I thought and got into the dress tugging on its fabric to provide me with as much cover as it could. The tugging continued through the auto ride and as we paid the cover charges to get into the club, but once inside it didn't take long for my inhibitions to disappear. The club had a large central hall with a dance floor, a bar and the DJ console. One side of the hall was lined up with see-through glass and opened into the lounge area which had comfortable sofas and settees for those who wished to sip their drinks in peace. The lounge area even had a separate bar counter lined up with tall barstools to service the patrons.

We were early for a Saturday evening and yet the place was fairly crowded. All seats in the lounge area were taken and there were people lurking about the bar counter as well, but a few of the stools were yet to be occupied. We proceeded towards the counter and perched upon two of the corner stools.

A brief glimpse of the surroundings and I felt like Virgin Mary, not the drink but the Virgin herself, and for good reason. The gender ratio in the club was heavily skewed towards females and most of them were clad in flimsy nothings making me feel as comfortable in my dress as I would have, had I been draped in a Saree. If there was one place in the city I could never imagine visiting with my folks, it was this. My father would have run the risk of a cardiac arrest while my mother, in all likelihood, would have renounced this morally dilapidated world and sought solace on some obscure peak of the Himalayas.

We ordered for a peg of Vodka each and began chatting up, comparing the carefree lives we led in the city to the constrained ones we had managed to escape from. It was nice to be talking freely with her, much like the old times, something we had been missing out on lately. 'So, do you have some interesting men at your workplace?' she suddenly enquired. Back in Rajkot, though we shared almost every other thing with each other, such topics were usually not broached so casually.

But then, a lot had changed since then. Barely a couple of months back I could hardly imagine myself sitting at a club bar, wearing a scanty dress and carelessly sipping on a glass of Vodka. 'Nothing much, just the usual crowd,' I said, and even as I did, I felt Ravi's face suddenly flash before my eyes.

'Hmmm, you know, you were never a great liar. Out with it, come on… who is he?' Something about the way I had replied must have given away my hesitation and she was quick to latch on.

'Well, there is nothing going on between us… but I think I am sort of fond of him,' I replied sheepishly.

'Wow, that's fabulous news!' she exclaimed. 'What's his name? And does he share the same fondness for you as well?'

'He hasn't said so in as many words, but I think he also likes me. Ravi, that's his name and don't be surprised but he is my boss,' I replied with a smile.

'Not bad at all. So, you gunned for the boss straight up? When do I get to meet him?'

'Hold your horses, sweetheart. As I said, he hasn't said anything or expressed his feelings to me as yet and once he does, rest assured, you will be the first person I will make him meet. Happy?'

'Cool, but it is fabulous news. I think we must drink to it,' she said, turning towards the bartender. 'Excuse me… can you help us with two Tequila shots please?' I contemplated a refusal. After all I had barely just heard about Tequila, and what I had heard of it did not leave me with much courage to risk consuming it. But the palpable eagerness on Kamini's face prevented me from voicing my concerns and I was soon holding a miniature glass filled with the tawny liquid.

Aping her actions I applied some salt on the webbing of my hand, picked up a slice of lime and gulped the Tequila, following it up with a quick nibble of the salt and a generous squeeze of lemon. My face had not even recovered from the distortion due to the bitter, sour and salty taste in my mouth, and the burning sensation I could feel all the way from my throat to the tummy when a deep-set husky voice called out to us.

'Excuse me! Don't I know you from somewhere?' I turned around to find the origin of the voice, a well-built man in his late twenties, staring straight back at us. Thankfully his question was directed towards Kamini and not me. How lame, I thought, the line was outdated even by Rajkot standards, let alone for being used in an up-market Mumbai club. I turned back glancing towards my friend who was now sizing up the intruder, feigning an effort on her memory. 'Maybe at Rahul's party?' he added for her benefit.

'Oh, yes! Indeed, at Rahul's party! How could I forget! Hi, I am Kamini,' she said, extending her hand towards the intruder. 'Of course I remember you. I am Harshad,' he said, reaching out to grab her extended hand. Maybe I was wrong and he actually was one of Kamini's acquaintances, I mused. He then waved towards someone in the crowd – the place was now buzzing, leaving the patrons with barely enough space to stand without rubbing shoulders with each other - and another man walked up to join us. 'This is my friend Rohan,' Harshad introduced him to us, as Kamini went on to assist them with my introduction.

Rohan, we learnt, was an actor and had played itsy-bitsy character roles in some recently released movies. I could not recollect having seen him on screen, but anyways I hadn't been watching too many films lately. Harshad, on the other hand, was a businessman and owned a chain of Spas in the city.

The drinks must have been telling their worth, for soon we were chatting like long lost friends – sharing jokes and guffawing incessantly, sharing high-fives and even teasing each other. Both men were interesting and kept us amused with their witty anecdotes and humorous one-liners. It was only when the bartender announced the last orders for the evening that I glanced at my watch. It was 1.00 a.m. and barring the brief visits to the ladies room, we had been sitting on the same stools for over four hours. And surprisingly I wasn't quite ready to go back just as yet.

'Get us the check please,' Kamini instructed the bartender, only to be cut short by Harshad. 'Hold on! Repeat one round of drinks for us all and put their bill on my tab,' he directed instead. We voiced our protest, first to Harshad and then to the bartender, but neither seemed to be listening. As instructed, the tender served us the drinks and flashing a teasing smile towards us, handed the check to Harshad for signing. He was clearly a regular here and there was no chance that the bartender would act against his wishes and side with us first timers instead. So we watched meekly as, displaying an exceptional and rare act of chivalry, Harshad signed for the drinks we had consumed through the evening.

'It is stupid how they force the clubs to shut down so early. You girls interested in heading somewhere else to grab a few more drinks?' Rohan enquired as we sipped on our last drinks for the evening at Fusion. 'But where can we go now?' Kamini reasoned. I had some random thoughts sprouting within my head too, but finding myself unable to cast them into words, I settled for the role of a silent spectator. I had stopped counting my drinks after four Vodkas and the one Tequila, which too seemed like hours ago.

'Well, if you are fine with it, we could head to my place. Except for the one servant, there is no one in the house. It is barely a five minute drive and we can booze in peace there,' Harshad suggested. And before we knew, all four of us were staggering towards the exit keeping each other from bumping into things, animate or inanimate, along the way.

'How do you know this fellow... Harshad?' I slurred into Kamini's ear as we waited for his car in the portico. 'From Rahul's party,' she whispered back.

'But, who the fucking hell is Rahul?'

'I don't know,' she shrugged. 'But who the fuck cares?' she added with a wink, lazily raising her hand to give me a high-five. It was indeed amusing. I tried to respond, lifting my own hand and hurling it towards her but found it slicing through the air to come back and strike me on my thighs. Both of us started laughing – a loud, meaningless and continual chuckle - as the patrons emerging from the club stared towards us in amazement. Just then Harshad's shining blue beamer surfaced ahead and he held the door open for us to get in. We continued to laugh mindlessly till the car came to a screeching halt in front of a modern, expensive-looking building.

I could barely open my eyes and the tearing pain in my head was viciously spreading to various other parts of my body. My lids were heavy and my limbs too were reeling under a spent feeling. As I struggled to open my eyes and lift myself from the bed, I stumbled back holding my head. It felt abnormally heavy, as though one half of my brain had suddenly turned to steel.

I closed my eyes once again and after a brief pause started opening them back slowly. I was surprised to find myself lying on my own bed. I had absolutely no recollection of how I had managed to get back. I turned and was partly relieved to find a human form sprawled next to me. It was Kamini and she was sound asleep. Next I glanced towards the table clock; it was 2.00 o'clock in the afternoon.

I massaged my temples and tried pressing my memory to extract as much of the happenings from the last evening as I could. I remembered being ushered by Harshad into his flat, a richly decorated and tastefully furnished one. Next, I remembered someone handing me a glass, it wasn't Vodka, Whiskey maybe. As the memories reluctantly began to stream, I started coughing. There was a certain soreness I could feel in my throat. It must have been the smoke.

Yes, I had smoked too and it wasn't a cigarette. The stick wasn't very symmetrical, much like an abstraction rolled in a kids art class. Weed, yes that's what he had referred to it as! I couldn't recall as to which of the two boys it had been though. Kamini had taken a few long drags and passed it on. Once again I had emulated her actions, only to be overcome by a bout of coughing. Yes, I had coughed then too.

I could also feel a mild, tingling pain in my breasts and between my legs. It had been subdued by the hammer-like throbbing I could feel in my head, but I knew that it was there. I felt one breast and then the other - yes, it was much more pronounced when touched. Slowly, I eased one of them from the dress and the bra-cup and lifted my head slightly to look at it. At two places, extremely close to the nipples, I could see distinct red abrasions – love bites, I thought.

I vaguely remembered Rohan toying with them with his hand and his mouth. But at the same time I had a similar recollection about Harshad as well. A hazy image of his bare chest thumping against mine was trying to materialize in my head. Then suddenly it stuck me like a bolt of lightening with a brutal, almost physical force – an orgy, that's what it had been.

As the enormity of the events dawned upon me, I started to cry. Initially it was merely streams of tears tricking down my eyes, but within minutes I was howling and convulsing on the bed, like a little child who had broken her favorite toy. It was like an attack of hysterical panic on steroids and I had no option but to flow along, like… like I had done the last evening.

My priced possession had been shattered and the only recollection I had of the ordeal was murky and obscure. I had lost my virginity and I did not know which of the two men was responsible. I was certain that I had made out with both but I had no idea as to which of them had been the first. I felt like a slut, a prostitute who sleeps with any willing customer – only in their case they still have a purpose; they do it for the money.

'Seju… What happened?' The voice and a hand I felt patting my head jerked me away from my thoughts. I was disgusted. I wanted to be left alone and I wanted no physical contact with anyone, let alone Kamini. She was my friend, someone I trusted and she had allowed all this to happen. 'Don't,' I screamed, pushing her away with as much force as I could muster.

'Hey, come on. It is ok, such things happen. Why are you reacting so fiercely?' she tried to reason.

'What happens? Just, what happens? Tell me… Do you even realize as to what has happened? We fucked complete strangers, people that we had barely met a couple of hours back. Hell, we don't even know their surnames… and you say 'it happens'? How could you?' I said before the words were dissolved within my loud sobbing.

Realizing that in my current state I was way beyond the scope for a discussion, Kamini left the room to return with two cups of tea. 'Here, have this. This will make you feel better,' she said. I did not touch the brew. I was troubled. No matter how hard I tried to peel my thoughts away from the episode, the images kept coming back to me laden with fresh pangs of guilt.

I had no idea when, weighed down by a numbing exhaustion, I slipped into the grasp of sleep and for how long I had been crying prior to that, but when I got up the room was enveloped in an eerie darkness. Supporting my head with one hand, I made an attempt to get up. The sleep had helped in reducing the heaviness and the stinging ache considerably and with a little effort I was able to switch on the lights. With measured steps I dragged myself to the washroom.

I was still wearing Kamini's dress which in its crumpled and creased state was barely a glimpse of its former splendor, much like my own self. I took off the dress, only to realize that my satin panty – one of the two expensive ones I had - was missing. Immediately I felt my eyes going moist again. I hoped that the tears were an expression of my grief for the lost garment. I didn't want my thoughts drifting back to last night. I wasn't ready to undergo the ordeal all over again, so I turned on the shower and stepped under it.

After washing and scrubbing my body for a good twenty minutes when I emerged from the bathroom I was feeling much lighter. Kamini, who had possibly dozed off on one the chairs in the hall, followed me to the bedroom. She kept staring at me with eyes that betrayed gloom, despair and guilt, without speaking at word.

'How did we get back here?' it was I who eventually broke the silence. 'His folks were to return today morning so he got his driver to drop us early in the morning,' she replied.

'Means, they know where we stay?' I shot back. 'No… no… I had waited for the car to leave before entering the gate. So while the driver knows the area, he doesn't know the building that we stay in.'

'How could you… How could you let this happen?' I broke down once again, only this time when Kamini reached out and hugged me, I didn't push her back. 'I am sorry. I too was sloshed and didn't know what was happening. But relax now and let it be. Don't think about what happened.'

'How can I not think about what happened? I feel like a whore… On one side I claim to be in love with Ravi and on the other, I end up making out with two complete strangers. I feel terrible… What if Ravi was to find out?' I replied.

'Just because you made out with someone does not make you a slut. By that definition almost all men and most women around us should be termed as whores and the city, a big brimming brothel. God did not make humans to be monogamous and to feel sexually attracted to someone from the other gender is only natural. There is absolutely no shame in following your natural instincts and that is all you have done. How is this different from what happened between you and Jacob in Rajkot? Was that acceptable only because you knew him to be Nirav's friend or was it fine because you guys didn't go all the way? Who decides this limit, the degree of physical proximity it takes to breach the frontiers of morality?'

'You knew about Jacob and me?' I was taken aback at the revelation.

'Yes I did, but I didn't speak to you about it because you never brought it up. Obviously I didn't want to put you through any kind of embarrassment.'

'But I hadn't met Ravi back then. And as you said, it was only harmless exploring and we hadn't actually made out. What if… what if… one of them had some sort of a disease, or worse, what if I am pregnant? I wouldn't even know which one of the two is response for it?' I argued.

'Both of them had protection. Don't worry, they have their own safety to consider when making out with girls they too had barely met, so they would never have taken such a chance,' she said, and before I could react, continued, 'As for Ravi. What he doesn't know will not trouble him. Anyways you guys are not going around just as yet. Plus, how do you know that he hasn't been spending his weekends frolicking with other girls?'

'No, he isn't that type,' I was quick to rebut.

'Well, whatever little I know of men, you can't be sure about any of them. They don't hesitate in using power, money or any other influence they might have for the sake of a romp. Even the ones who seem most devoted to their partners don't hesitate in floundering a bit when their partners are not looking. I am not saying that Ravi is like that, but you surely don't need to worry yourself to death over something that happened before you had committed to him. Just like you should not be concerned about all that he did in his past life.'

'Men are different; no one goes about berating them if they are promiscuous. It isn't the same for us. Imagine what our parents will go through if they came to know about any of this? My father and Uncle (her father) too, I am sure, would commit suicide,' I continued.

'This is the biggest problem I have. If men digress, it is attributed to their 'need for a change' or plain and simple 'fun' whereas when women do the same things, they are branded as whores. And it is no one but we women ourselves who are responsible for establishing this duality of standards. Look around you! Times have changed. Women are walking step-by-step with men in every conceivable walk of life. We are no longer mere domesticated animals, dependant on men for all our worldly needs. Why then should we cringe at the thought of doing something that we feel like doing? While you are sitting here cursing yourself over what happened, do you think those two are even giving it a second thought? If anything, they would only be boasting about it as their latest conquest among their friends. Why shouldn't we at least look at it as a night gone by and move on?'

Suddenly Kamini seemed to be fuming and her words were backed by a conviction that had been absent in the discussion thus far.

Maybe her angst was a result of some prejudice she had been subject to – possibly something to do with Nirav - but speculations or confrontations were not what I was seeking. I had ample of counter arguments still bubbling within me but at the same time I desperately wanted to believe every word of what she was saying. It didn't matter whether I was convinced or whether I was still reeling under the guilt of my actions. What mattered was that I had a life ahead of me and if I was to give myself any chance of facing it with gusto, I had to leave the baggage of this one mishap behind me.

The next day I called Ravi and informed him that I wasn't well and would not be coming to work. 'Why? What happened?' the concern in his voice was apparent and it resulted in an instinctive smile surfacing on my face. 'Nothing serious, just head ache – migraine probably. I should be back in office tomorrow,' I replied.

Kamini had some errands to attend and so she left right after breakfast whereas I retired to the bed once again. I mulled over the things she had said, her arguments and points of view and repeated them over and over again in my head. I wasn't a whore. It was a mistake that had been committed and there was no point in mulling over it indefinitely. I had to move on.

SIX

It took me some time, but soon the penitent episode, like a dreadful nightmare, was behind me. I was glad that neither Harshad nor Rohan had attempted to establish contact with us and my mind had craftily managed to reduce their existence to near-fictitious characters whose role in my life could not be accurately established.

At the workplace too, the tides appeared to be taking a favorable turn and the performance pressure too was easing out. Ravi had continued to act as my interim partner and with his expertise achieving targets was no longer as intricate a task as it had initially been. He had slowly eased me into responding to customer queries and dealing with them on my own. The hand-holding had done a world of good for my professional development and inner confidence.

Chatu, as expected, had not mended his ways and instead chosen to part with the company once his three month probation was over. A new employee, Siddhesh, was inducted in his place and paired with me. Only, now I was the senior partner. I was disappointed initially, since a likely implication of this was that I would get considerably lesser time to spend with Ravi, but soon I realized that my fears were unfounded.

Ravi too seemed to be missing my company as much and he made it a point to accompany us for calls once or twice in a week. In the evenings whenever he spotted me in office, he would offer to drop me back and I would readily accept. We would halt on the way for coffee, Kala Khatta or any other thing that could serve as an excuse for us to spend some time with each other. But like all budding relationships at the workplace, ours too was marred by the inhibition that came with the association we shared at work.

He being my boss meant that I had to be wary of what I said to him and so, despite there being a strong desire to express my feelings I had managed to keep them bottled within me. He too seemed to be struggling with a similar tussle, for, though his eyes revealed much more our discussions scarcely strayed beyond the routinely mundane themes. We spoke about work, we spoke about the weather, we spoke about people at work, we spoke about movies, but the one topic we continued to avoid like plague was what we felt about each other.

Just after completing my first year in Mumbai I decided to visit my folks back home in Rajkot. The initial turbulence had now settled and I was thriving in the frantic pace and the non-interfering way of life that the city offered. I had of course been regular with my calls home, but then there were times when I did miss the comforting presence of my parents and not to mention the gastronomical delights produced within the walls of my mother's kitchen.

If there was one person who had been left untouched by the all-encompassing telecom revolution in the country, it was my mother. She was yet to emerge from the days that people queued up outside STD booths to call their near and dear ones and an STD call for her was nothing more than a money-guzzling conspiracy hatched by the telecom companies in connivance with the government. She had taken it upon herself to offer resistance to the scam and hence irrespective of which side the call originated, she ensured that it didn't last a millisecond beyond the necessary. My calls too had to bear the brunt of her idiosyncrasies and were forced to remain short and to the point, making me feel further distanced from home and my craving to visit further strengthened.

So within days of the idea emerging in my head, I had applied for a week long leave and boarded the first available bus to Rajkot. The first few days at home barely left me with any breathing space as I shuffled between Kamini's and my own house delivering the presents that we had both shopped and reinforcing our well-being to both set of eager parents. The erstwhile sleepy city seemed to have woken up from its slumber and become a center of frenzy in my absence, allowing my mother to accumulate a truck load of gossip to update me with. I too was carrying my own baggage to download, a carefully censured version though.

Once the verbal transactions were accomplished, I suddenly started to find myself engulfed by boredom. Maybe I had outgrown Rajkot or maybe I had simply lost touch with my roots, but strangely I was missing Mumbai and my life back there. Even more surprising was the fact that of all things and people I had left behind, Ravi was on my mind the most. I was missing our conversations, the bike rides and his sheer presence around me. On my third night at home, I was sprawled on my bed, thinking about Ravi and smiling to myself when my mobile phone began to beep. I smiled looking at the name that was flashing on the screen. 'Eerie,' I thought as I received the call.

'Hi Ravi... What a pleasant surprise! How are you?'

'I am fine... just the same as I was when you left. You tell me, how is everything at home?' he responded casually. For a few minutes he kept beating around the bush talking about inconsequential matters from work and then he finally said it, 'You know there is something I needed to tell you. Actually I have been deliberating over it for quite some time but kept avoiding bringing it up since I wasn't sure of your reaction. Not that much has changed in that regard but your absence made me realize that I would probably be better off speaking it out rather than intensifying my agony by holding it within.'

Pause! He was waiting for me to respond, I guess. 'That's OK, you don't have to be scared of me. Tell me, what is it?' I said, struggling to feign ignorance while another part of me was busy preempting the words he would speak next. I was guilty of keeping my own feelings bottled for way too long and that was adding to my anxiety.

'You know, I think I kind of like you. And I was wondering as to what do you think about me?' he hesitantly muttered.

'Is this what you wanted to say? Obviously, I like you too, otherwise why would we remain such great friends,' I responded. I was excited and it was perhaps the excitement that was responsible for the sudden surge in my confidence levels. I was enjoying being in the position of control and not to mention the perverse pleasure I was deriving out of teasing him.

'Not like that. Of course, we are friends but… but I was referring to something else. I mean, I don't know how you would take this but I think I am falling in love with you. It's barely been a few days since you left and it already seems like eternity. I miss you Sejal and I want to be with you, now and forever.'

I could feel a giddy something in my stomach and my heart seemed to be beating at a record-breaking pace. I wanted to jump up and down and do all sorts of crazy things, but with great difficulty I checked myself. 'Oh! See Ravi, you are a treasured friend and an amazing person. Any girl would love to have you as her companion but just that I have never really thought about you in that fashion. I think I will need some time to think,' I said instead. I had seen enough movies and read enough books to know that a girl, no matter how eager she was, should not come across as too easy to get.

I returned to Mumbai on a Sunday morning and as I alighted from the Bus, I was pleasantly surprised to find Ravi standing on the pavement across the road, flashing his 1000 watt smile. I glanced at my watch; it was 6.00 a.m., hardly a time to be out of the bed, let alone for standing on the road and waiting for a bus.

Since his first call he had been calling me on a daily basis and we had continued to chat as though he had never proposed. We had both conveniently stashed the conversation somewhere in the background for the time being. Last evening, before I boarded the bus, we had spoken briefly and I had shared my travel schedule with him but the last thing I had been expecting was to see him waiting for me at the bus stand. I was thrilled but once again I chose not to exhibit my excitement and instead resorted to complaining about the needlessness of the gesture.

However, this one gesture of his was enough to erase any doubts about our relationship that could have been lingering within me. I was now sure that Ravi was the man for me, one who would go to great lengths for my sake, and I was anxious for him to pop the question again so that I could respond with a resounding yes. But the chance never came. Perhaps my body language and actions had betrayed my emotions and in no time we were acting and behaving like a couple without any formal acknowledgements.

Though unstated, both of us knew that any word of our relationship reaching the office would be detrimental for our respective careers and so we consciously kept our liaisons outside the periphery of the premises. When at work, we confined ourselves to only the most basic and essential exchanges and he continued to drop me home from work, only the barrier of formality now having lifted from the act. He no longer offered the lift wrapped in excuses about how he was 'anyways passing by that side' and I refrained from exhibiting my customary reluctance.

In the evenings we would go to the beach, a park, a restaurant or any other place that allowed us enough privacy to hold hands and exchange sweet whispers or sometimes progress a step or two beyond as well. One such hang-out that I particularly favored was Bandra Bandstand. The park near the Bandra Fort or even the promenade itself served as a rendezvous point for many an aching hearts.

The area wasn't particularly private but the numerous couples who seemed lost in their own world, oblivious to the scrutiny of the passer-bys, offered a unique sense of comfort and coziness. Everything was simple; the degree of coziness you could engage in was a function of the amount you paid to the policeman who was bound to walk up to you at some point. For a hundred rupees you could sit there holding hands and engage in light petting without being disturbed - but for the occasional vendor who might attempt to lure you with a packet of wafers or a soft drink - and for double the amount you could even engage in the heavier, more passionate stuff.

For me it wasn't so much about an opportunity to engage in physicality, but the serene and romantic ambience that did the trick. The diverse faces, cutting across social boundaries that converged on the Bandstand every evening made it seem like a gala fest for lovers and I was glad to be a part of it.

Living up to my promise I invited Ravi over to our flat one evening and introduced him to Kamini. The two hit it off instantly and I was glad at that. 'Nice guy, mature and sensible!' Kamini voiced her approval after meeting him. Her approval meant that he no longer remained off-bounds from our flat like most other men. And once in a while he did come up for a quick cup of coffee, but his visits remained sporadic and short since he wasn't particularly comfortable visiting a flat habited by two single girls.

I couldn't quite comprehend his inhibitions since I quite enjoyed spending time at his place in Powai. It was a two bedroom apartment that Ravi shared with two of his friends, a typical bachelor's pad with garments ranging from dirty socks and underwear to denims and shirts strewn randomly at every conceivable vantage point. In fact I had myself rescued the poor television from doubling up as a clothes-line on numerous occasions. The kitchen was functional but barely used since the boys usually ate out on their way back from work.

Like Kamini, Ravi's roommates too warmed up to me in no time, addressing me as Bhabhi and making clumsy quick-fix efforts at tidying up the place whenever I was visiting. A chair was excavated from within a pile of clothing, a glass – often steel but sometimes even plastic - was identified from the debris around and I was made to sit comfortably and offered water to drink. I loved their awkward expressions of affection and reciprocated by cooking for them or tidying up the house whenever I could. I relished the role of the lady of the house and it appeared as though not only Ravi but his roommates too looked forward to my visits.

I could imagine the warm motherly affection that Snow White would have felt towards her seven dwarfs, only I had three and they were not even close to qualifying for dwarfs. In time I found myself spending most of my weekends at Ravi's place. It was as though I had found a surrogate family of adolescents whose upkeep had naturally become my responsibility. Whenever I was staying over, the other two, if they were home, permitted Ravi and me to use the only bedroom that had a bed and slept on the floor in the other room instead.

Ravi wasn't a party animal and preferred sipping a drink at home instead of visiting a club or a bar. 'Why spend so much for one little peg when for the same amount you can buy a whole bottle for yourself. As for the music, I can play the same numbers for you at home,' he claimed. But I still managed to drag him to one of the nightspots every now and then, usually one that came heavily recommended by Kamini.

During this period, among a host of other things in my life, even my wardrobe had undergone a complete revamp and had started to somewhat resemble Kamini's. A lot of my Salwar Suits had been replaced with trousers, skirts and shirts. My casual attires too had expanded beyond the perfunctory denims and t-shirts and now included pedal pushers, shorts and dresses. I even had a little black dress of my own now, one that was as glamorous as the one that I had borrowed from my roommate for our first night out. I had completely transformed from the small-town girl to a big-city belle, but for my name which stuck out like a sore souvenir of my orthodox Gujarati antecedents.

Sejal… my parents would have had to hate me immensely for doing this. They could have named me anything… anything but for following the typical Gujarati method of picking up a few random syllables and affixing 'al' as a suffix to arrive at a girl's name. Hetal, Bejal, Sejal, Jinal and Deepal put together, I was sure, would account for a majority of the female population within the community. I even remembered a girl called Anal, Anal Shah or something, from school. Imagine having to lead a life giving all your detractors a right to address you as 'Anal' at their whims and fancies. My parents had been marginally better off with their creativity, but the name was still a stereotypical annotation I could do without.

Anyways, there was little I could do about that now. Surprisingly though, Ravi seemed to have an inexplicable affinity for my name and on my birthday went on to gift me a pendant that had the letters S E J A L neatly carved in gold. I rarely ever wore it.

Like the pendant, there were various others contentious but minute issues that kept cropping up once in a while in our otherwise smooth affair. But then, what is a relationship without its fair share of tiffs? The important thing was that none of our altercations lasted beyond a day or two and the subsequent days were usually the dreamiest ones with both of us making that tad bit of extra effort to appease the other.

Ravi was usually the one to initiate the patch up and he had his own charming ways of doing so. One time that I distinctly remember was when he had written a poem for me after an argument, the reason for which I had forgotten even while the sulking phase had lasted. It went something like this:

Life for me had always been the same,
Joy when happy and sorrow when in pain!
Then suddenly, into my life you came…
And its very meaning began to change.

I know now what real happiness means,
And why every morning, the lonely bird sings.
It's you and only you my sweetheart,
Who, like an adjective, defines my soul and heart!

I am certain that this is not the end,
I am only human and I shall err again.
But with every tear of yours I feel a numbing pain,
That makes me swear to never trouble you again.

With these lines that I am jotting down,
Like a looney freak I might begin to sound.
But the only thing I know is for sure,
That with each passing day I shall love you even more.

Kamini had been in splits on reading his feeble attempt at poetry but for me it was something priceless and treasured. The thought of being the motivation behind any creation of art, celebrated or otherwise, is simply fantastic. Every time I read the lines, I found myself in the same zone of elation that Mona Lisa or Mumtaz Mahal would have scaled at some point in time, a zone that left no scope for petty grudges and inconsequential sulking.

Life in Ravi's company seemed like a breeze and as each day strode along, culminating into weeks and months, I found myself flowing uninhibitedly treasuring each moment for its worth. Asleep and awake, during the most sublime and abject moments, I would think about him and when together, we would reminisce our past, relish the present and recapitulate about our future – our marriage, our kids, their names, our house and the color of its walls and who would be in-charge of doing up the interiors.

However, lost in the world of my dreams, I seemed had overlooked a very crucial fact of life. The fact that every peak is followed by a trough and that bliss is not but punctuation between the distress and grief that density has charted out for each one of us to endure. I had missed out on spotting the maleficent dark clouds looming, as is so often the case and when I fell, I fell hard and flat on my face.

SEVEN

'I was not prepared for this. I didn't know what to do. Why aren't you saying something? Speak up, will you,' the agitation in his voice was apparent, only it was relatively mild in comparison with the disturbance I could feel welling up within me. I chose to remain silent.

We were sitting at the Worli Sea face and were engaged in a discussion that was to determine the fate of our relationship. Well, it wasn't exactly a discussion since I had barely uttered a word for the last fifteen minutes, still reeling under the shock that I had been confronted with.

It was only a month back that we had completed two blissful years of our being together. Ravi had organized a small celebration at his place, the guest-list including Kamini, his two roommates and a couple of other friends. It was a fun evening with music, drinks and dance and not to forget the sleek I Pod that he had bought as my present.

Later, when the guests left, leaving the house looking like a field rummaged by a herd of wild buffaloes, I could not but employ myself in an attempt at its resurrection. A slightly tipsy Kamini was staring at me, hoping that I would come off my cleaning spree and head home. She was tired and it showed. 'Why don't we stay back? You don't have to leave for work till late in the evening tomorrow. We can catch some sleep and head back home early in the morning,' I offered in an attempt to assuage her tussle with sleep.

She immediately agreed and we put up a make shift bed for her on the drawing room floor. Within minutes she passed out emitting an incessant muzzled humming. Ravi's roommates had retired too, finally providing us with an opportunity for a private celebration. I looked at him, he was staring right back at me. I knew what was playing on his mind and when he opened his mouth to say something, I knew it was to invite me to our bedroom. I was eager for the privacy too.

'Want to go down for a stroll to the Powai Lake? It looks fascinating at night,' he said instead. I was slightly taken aback. A boy and a girl, both a few drinks down, an empty room with no other conscious soul in the house and he was thinking about going for a stroll? I looked at my watch, 2.00 a.m. I had office to attend the next morning and that after a quick pit-stop at home. 'He has office too and what the heck, he is my boss,' I thought. 'Ok, let's go,' I found myself saying.

He hadn't been exaggerating. The lake was a sight to see with lights from various sources reflecting on its shivering waters, blues and reds from neon signages, the yellow from the street lights and the white and golden from nearby residential high-rises. The usually busy promenade was deserted and the silence was only making the view even more mesmerizing. 'Fabulous,' I muttered, as he guided me down the slight slope that took us away from the road and closer to the water.

Still in awe of the magical vista, I was leaning on the rails staring at nothing in particular when I felt Ravi's hands on my waist and his chin on my right shoulder. He had walked up behind me to hold me in an embrace. 'You were looking lovely today,' he whispered. 'Only today?' I teased, but as I turned to look at him, I found my lips perilously close to his. I could feel his warm breath bouncing off me and the slight quiver of his lips was too tempting to resist. I reached out for them with my own and we were soon clasped in a passionate lip-lock.

We were in a public place at an unearthly hour and reeking with alcohol. The Powai police station was barely a few yards away and the lake with its utility as a dump for evidence – previously breathing or otherwise - pertaining to various sorts of crimes was a more than likely spot for a surprise inspection. And yet, unmindful of the risks involved, we continued to explore each other fervidly.

One thing led to the next and soon we were undulating on the concrete floor of the walk-way completely ignorant of anything else around us. My top and skirt were bunched up somewhere around my waist and we were making out under the sky and stars in full view of anyone who dared to venture a few steps beyond the main road. Obviously the fear of being caught was there at the back of our minds, but it was acting more as a catalyst for the fire we were burning under rather than working towards dousing it. The thrill of living on the edge or the excitement of indulging in the prohibited, whatever it was, it only made the experience more adventurous and before we realized, everything came to a sudden shuddering halt.

We remained glued to each other for a few more minutes until the abrasions our little game had resulted in on my back started to make their presence felt with burning sensation and a mild pain. Slowly we got up, tending to our now-shabby clothes and started to walk back home with a smile of content and satisfaction.

'We must get married soon,' I thoughtlessly uttered.

'Will you believe this; I was thinking the exact same thing. Isn't that supposed to be a sign of good luck?' he replied. Ravi did not want to tell his folks about me telephonically so he planned a trip to his hometown to be able to discuss our marriage with them in person.

He called me and we chatted briefly on his first night home; he hadn't spoken to his parents till then. The next day, following his instructions, I waited for his call till late in the evening and when it didn't come, I dialed his number; the call went unanswered. After a couple of attempts, I stopped trying and left a text message for him instead. 'I am worried! Tried reaching you several times but couldn't. Please call when you get this.'

After another hour or so, I got a reply from him stating that all was well and since he wasn't in a position to talk then, he would share the details of his chat with his parents upon his return. I heaved a sigh of relief. Not that I was expecting anything untoward, but the sudden freeze in communication had my thoughts racing untamed.

He had called me early today morning, probably on his way to office from the bus stand, and asked me to meet up for coffee after work. He sounded normal, we even chatted briefly about return journey and the few arbitrary incidents that had occurred in office during his absence, but his coffee invite seemed somewhat strange. We were a couple and he had come back to town after three days; it was only obvious that I would be going out with him. There wasn't any need for that special invite.

I should have taken a hint then or maybe when I didn't bump into him at work even once during the entire day, but the day had been particularly busy and the excitement of meeting him was playing on my mind throughout. Therefore, it came as an unexpected shock when he dealt the blow as soon as we took a table at the coffee shop. 'I don't know how to say this,' he started sounding hesitant, and after a brief pause he added, 'I have got engaged.'

It was too sudden; I took a few moments to comprehend the meaning that the assortment of words held in their midst; I looked for an omitted punctuation or an error in sentence formulation that could have altered the meaning of what he wished to convey, I found none. 'What are you saying? How?' I finally heard myself speak. The words were not as high pitched as I would have liked them to be. In fact they didn't seem to be coming from me at all. It was as though I had been transported to a different plane and was witnessing the exchange from a distance as a neutral observer. My mind was totally numb.

'I told my father that I loved you and wanted to get married to you,' he began. The past tense he used in defining his feelings for me did not go unnoticed. 'He obviously had issues… the caste, society and all that. He told me that he had already committed my hand in marriage to a business associate for his daughter and wanted me to meet her instead. I declined and stormed out of the scene.' He waited for a reaction; I gave him none. What did he expect? An accolade or something! I knew the eventual outcome of the discussion and yet he expected me to cheer his bravado even in light of its disastrous outcome.

'My reaction proved too much for him to endure and instantly he broke into a sweaty fit and started convulsing, holding his heart. I was scared. I rushed back to help him and even in his ailing state he refused to allow me to even touch him. I had betrayed him, he said, and since his misery did not matter to me, I should not touch him and express fake concern. I had no option but to give in to what he wanted; he seemed to be dying,' he continued, once again halting to look at me. As I bored back into his eyes, he quickly averted his gaze.

'I was not prepared for this. I didn't know what to do. Why aren't you saying something? Speak up, will you,' pause, 'What did you expect me to do? I couldn't let my dad die, could I?' his intonation shifted from anger to frustration to a near pleading one. I was unmoved. I could however feel a deep sense of loathing brewing within me for all that he was saying, all that he stood for and all that we had shared over the past couple of years.

I wasn't sure if it was him or his father who was inspired by some C-grade Bollywood film, but the bull he was trying to feed me was undoubtedly inspired by celluloid. An ailing father, a son, his love interest, the father's ultimate weapon to make his son surrender his love – a heart attack - it was funny in an extremely morose sort of a way. I didn't laugh, I didn't cry, maybe some part of me was still hoping that it was all a big joke and he would soon burst out laughing. 'How is uncle feeling now?' I found myself saying, finally breaking my self-inflicted silence.

'He is better. In fact, his health started to improve as soon as I gave in to his wishes,' he replied. He seemed relieved that the doors of communication had once again opened.

'So, in the one day that was left, you managed to get engaged as well?' I enquired, more for the sake of saying something than seeking an answer. The words were reeking with sarcasm, which, strangely he failed to identify. 'It wasn't exactly an engagement. We had this small ceremony called Roka, where the boy, the girl and the two sets of parents give their consent to the match.'

I wasn't interested in knowing the weird rituals they followed in his family or sect or region, the conversation was weighing upon me and now I desperately wanted it to end. I didn't know what had been his motivation - money, dowry, or maybe the girl was simply better looking than I was or who knows, he might always have been in love with her and I could have been just a stop-gap arrangement whose time for disposal had come.

I tried to give him the benefit of doubt and attempted to believe his story but I just couldn't bring myself to doing it; there were simply too many loose ends to ignore. Yes, I was mildly curious about the girl – her name, what she did for a living, how she looked - but in the end it didn't seem worth the effort I would have had to make in listening to him speak about her. 'Then, that's it I guess?' I said, looking into his eyes, and without waiting for an answer, picked up my handbag and headed out of the coffee shop.

I heard him shout out my name a couple of times but thankfully we hadn't settled the bill yet and that prohibited him from following me out. I hailed the first form of conveyance I saw, a taxi, and rushed the driver into driving away from there. I was glad to be out of the coffee shop; only, then I had no clue about the gravity of the impression that this incident was to leave on my life to come.

'Madam, where to?' the taxi driver's question steered me away from my thoughts. He had popped the question twice already without eliciting a response, which explained the mild irritation in his tone. 'Marine Drive,' something prompted me to say; maybe the need to be near the sea or maybe the need to go as far away from Ravi as I could.

I spent an hour, maybe two, or even three, staring at the waves - starting small and then swelling up, only to crash inconsequentially against the boulders lining up the Marine Drive promenade. They seemed to be reciting the story of my own life to me; one of utter triviality and hitting dead-ends after dead-ends. I thought about Ravi, the joy he had brought along and the life I had been dreaming about with him, and I washed my thoughts away by streams of salty silent tears.

This was the beauty of the city; nobody here bothered about anyone else. People carried on with their lives – a group of young boys laughing and making merry, young couples holding hands and looking into each others dreamy eyes, and the odd vendor trying to sell the last of his stuff - mindless of the solitary girl trying to drown herself in her own tears. I mused whether any of them would even notice if I decided to jump into the vast expanse of water and bring my pitiful existence to its conclusion.

I wasn't nursing any serious thoughts about committing suicide so the sudden thought ended up scaring me out of my wits. Not meaning to mislead my mind, which seemed to have acquired the status of an independent activist of late, I got up and started walking away from the water. My phone started vibrating once again and this time I bothered myself with a quick glance on the screen. Kamu Calling, were the letters flashing on it. I disconnected and checked the missed call register; there were 7 calls from Kamini, 2 from Ravi and one from an unknown number.

'Where are you? When are you returning home? Ravi had called to check on you as well. Text me if you can't call,' an SMS from her lit up the screen just as I was about to surrender the phone into my bag. 'I am ok. Will be late,' I sent her a quick reply before putting it back in. It was almost midnight and though the vehicles on the road gave the city an appearance of being on the move still, a closer look revealed its definite progress towards a lethargic slumber. The number of people on marine drive as well as the streets had thinned out considerably and those who were around also seemed to be walking with a definitive purpose instead of generally loitering about. I felt like the only one who was drifting aimlessly and I wasn't ready to go back home just as yet.

I kept meandering through the streets of Old Bombay admiring the contrast it presented to my part of the city with its neat and planned streets, regal looking buildings and the affluent flavor it exuded. I passed through bright streets with road side stalls catering to the hungry, I scampered across dark alleys that cast a promise of impending disaster and I followed random turns and winding lanes, and just when I thought I had managed to lose myself completely and comprehensively, I emerged into a street which was very different from the Mumbai (or any other city for that matter) that I had known.

A well lit street, uncharacteristically pulsating for the given hour, lined up with small wooden doors and grilled windows greeted me. There were people, mostly men, observing and walking about, as if on a window-shopping spree at one of the suburban malls. What made the street different was that the wares they were shopping for were human, women to be precise. There were tens of them sticking out their heads and several other body parts from the doors and windows, making catcalls and lewd gestures to catch the attention of potential customers. They were all drenched in make-up - the bright, dazzling and cheap variety - and were clad in skirts, dresses and even blouse-petticoats sans the Saree.

The street, which I later learnt, was Kamathipura, the infamous red-light district of Mumbai; a nocturnal jaunt for the morally depraved and sexually obsessed. My curiosity was only momentary and soon, with the naked lust-laden looks I was garnering from both the customers and the wares, I found a chill of fear running down my spine. Turning back would have been too conspicuous, I couldn't afford to project that I was lost. The street anyways didn't seem too long, therefore I continued to walk, adding a spring of purpose to my strides, head bowed low, and stealing glances from the corner of my eyes.

A few times I thought as if someone was calling out to me but I continued walking without turning back and within minutes I was out of the 'action' end of the street. I heaved a sigh of relief and thanked all the deities whose names I had been silently chanting through the brief hike. I rushed to one of the waiting cabs and without waiting for the driver to react I got inside and slammed the door behind me. 'Andheri,' I almost screamed out my destination. I was ready to go home now.

All through the cab journey scenes that my subconscious had gathered kept flashing in front of my eyes – young girls, some of them barely in their early teens, garishly painted in pink and red, laughing, hooting and urging people to choose them over another; fat, ugly men with menacing looks surveying and examining them as though shopping for fish in the local fish market; and the colossal currents of pain and suffering that underlined every transaction that occurred on the street. Suddenly my own problems seemed dwarfed and as I got down from the cab, I recalled that for the past hour and half I had not thought about Ravi even once.

I had made a resolve to continue with life as though nothing had happened. I went to work, spoke with Ravi on matters that necessitated a consultation with the boss and returned home to the solace of my solitude. Initially, he made a few feeble attempts to engage me in conversation about the recent developments but I curtly sliced through them, steering myself clear of his efforts. If he wished to establish that what had happened was a circumstantial doing and he still deserved the erstwhile pedestal in my eyes, he was highly mistaken. And when the outcome was a given, what purpose was a discussion, a guilt-purging initiative for him, going to serve for me anyways?

But within a matter of days I realized the futility of my efforts. When you have truly loved someone it is not easy to close yourself to his existence and move on, especially when you continue to remain in his proximity. Soon the sore had settled and I had started look forward to catching a glimpse of Ravi or hearing his voice, even if it were his views on a client quotation or something equally mundane.

A part of me, which I think would be the rational side, was not happy with the tidings and wanted me to put a brake on my desires. I had burnt myself once already and while even a stupid cat had enough brains to not lick a vessel that had scorched it once, I was finding myself drawn to the very subject of my anguish. The tug-of-war waging within me was not helping at all. It left me thinking about things I believed to have been long buried and in the bargain it led me to start doubting my own sensibilities and strength.

Ravi in the meantime had given up making any efforts for a truce and this didn't help my cause either. Every time that he passed by without acknowledging my presence I felt a tearing pain run through my being. Over the days to follow I found myself living the life of a zombie, limiting my interactions with the outside world – Kamini and the calls to my parents included - barely concentrating on work or anything else that required my undivided attention. I could not watch a movie or a television program without thinking about Ravi and invariably he surfaced in my dreams even, further diluting my resolve.

The blissful life from barely a few weeks back had taken a blinding turn landing me in a dimensionless vacuum. I would find myself hoping that his roommates, my other two unruly kids, would manage to talk some sense into him and he would come back to me. I would wish that his fiancée would dump him for someone better or even that some Bollywood style clannish conflict would emerge between the two families making the marriage unfeasible, anything that could bring back my old life; and quickly I would jolt myself back to reality. No matter what flights of imagination I embarked upon, Ravi was not coming back to me; he was gone and I had to figure out a way to live with the fact.

EIGHT

'How long… just how long do you expect to survive like this? Don't you get it, he is history… past… gone! Men are like that only, phobic to commitment and highly opportunistic when it comes to relationships and women. Just get used to the fact. He enjoyed himself while the relationship lasted and so did you, so today when he has shut himself to the past and moved on, why can't you do the same?' Kamini had been dishing out the same spiel to me ever since my break-up.

The immediate cause for her outburst today was the invite to a movie premiere she had got from somewhere and was keen for me to accompany her. I had of course declined without giving it a second thought and thus invited her wrath upon me.

'You will not go out… not even watch a bloody movie; I don't understand what's got into you. Do you think he is also sitting there relishing the moroseness of life? No! It doesn't make a shit of a difference to his life if you sulk away the remainder of your own or end up in a mental asylum for that matter. I am not taking no for an answer. You are coming with me and that is final.'

Contrary to my expectations the outing turned out to be fun. It was an English film premiere and hence the usual Bollywood glitz was missing. Barring a few faces from the television industry there were no noteworthy faces that we could identify. Most of the gathering seemed to comprise of chance guests like us and we were soon at ease, devouring the free drinks and snacks and discussing the garments and accessories that the girls around were flaunting. I caught Kamini's fleeting glances pausing upon some of the men but I chose to ignore, I wasn't particularly curious about the race anymore. The movie too turned out to be entertaining and when we emerged from the theater I was feeling much lighter.

'Wanna stop by somewhere for a quick drink?' Kamini suggested. Memories of our first drinking spree were hazy but hadn't been completely washed, but I had learnt to handle my drinks much better since then. Plus I was feeling so relaxed after a long time and I wanted the feeling to last. 'Sounds good,' I replied.

'You remember Nirav?' she enquired abruptly. We had barely taken a few sips from our first drink, so I was sure that it wasn't the alcohol speaking for her. 'Of course I remember. What about him?' I responded. She had finally decided to talk and though the suspense wasn't exactly killing me, I was keen to know her story.

'I don't think I have loved anyone as much as I loved him. He was always there for me when I needed him and even when I did not. We shared some fantastic times together, especially after I came down to

Mumbai. Everything was as pleasant as I would have wanted it to be,' she began, slipping into the cloudy mist of her memories.

'His business of supplying shooting equipment to production houses was well established by the time I came here and he was making a decent bit of money. Our names were on the guest lists for most of the happening parties around town and his friend circle included many influential names from the television industry. To say the truth I was smitten by him all over again; by his lifestyle and his success. I had never even dreamt of leading such a life and when it presented itself as an eventuality, I had started to look forward to it. I loved going to parties and basking in the attention I garnered just by the virtue of being at his side. I was blinded by the dazzle and didn't see it coming.'

She was desperately controlling her tears from spilling while I sat silently not meaning to interfere with her long overdue outburst. 'I never would have believed it, had I not witnessed it myself. I never thought Nirav would do such a thing,' she continued, pausing intermittently for breath.

'He was in bed with two girls at the same time. I had dropped by at his place unannounced and since I had a set of the house keys, I hadn't bothered to check if he was home. I wanted to surprise him by cooking a meal and waiting for him when he returned. It was one of those days when I was at my romantic best and ironically I walked into his room to be greeted by the most despicable scene I could ever imagine. A woman, almost a decade older than us, was on top of him, riding with an animated screaming frenzy while another one, also stark naked, seemed to be egging them up. It was a disgusting visual, intolerable, and so I stormed out of the room and the house.'

Despite her precise description I could not bring myself to visualize Nirav, the decent, cultured guy I knew from Rajkot, in such a hideous situation. But who was I to judge him anyways? Hadn't I and Kamini too managed to land ourselves in a worse position? I however refrained from speaking my thoughts out aloud and continued to listen.

'I would have forgiven him; after all aren't we all prone to making errors? And when he came to my place later that evening, though still livid and disappointed, I had sobered down drastically. I was waiting for him to apologize but instead he went around justifying his actions. 'It happens,' he said. Apparently the lady was a chief production manager with one of his largest clients and had a bisexual orientation. 'These are little things that one has to do for survival. If I am to continue getting business from her, I have no option but to satisfy her needs, else there are a lot of people waiting to do much more for the sake of business,' he said.'

'I don't know if you understand Seju, but I was still the simple girl from Rajkot, who had been led by her heart to this city,' she spoke, briefly emerging from the fortress of her memories to acknowledge my presence. 'I understand,' I whispered with a nod.

'The side of Nirav I came across that day was very different from the one I had loved. The person in front of me was a materialistic stranger who could go to the most depressing of depths for the sake of achieving his material objectives. Back then I didn't know that this is how the world works and if you have to carve a place for yourself, you need to let go of redundant principles and values that we unknowingly cling on to. I clearly didn't understand a word of what he was saying and we ended up having our worst argument of all times. He shouted and so did I; I screamed and so did he; and then I don't know what happened to me and I hurled an empty glass at him, missing barely by a whisker. I only have a vague recollection of the exact sequence of events post that, but we were soon bundled up in a heap, tugging and pulling each others hair and throwing slaps and punches.'

I was aghast. I had seen little children engaging in fist fights, but two grown-ups, that too a boy and a girl entangled in a wrestle was beyond my imagination. 'You guys fought! As in fought, fought?' I asked, throwing a few imaginary punches of my own into thin air.

'Yes, at least for the few minutes it took him to overpower me. Anyways, that was the last I saw of him and though I know I might not have been completely blameless, I don't really have much regrets over what happened. It is only occasionally, like right now, that I end up getting swayed by my emotions,' she said, wiping the moisture in her eyes with the back of her hand. I reached out and gave her a tight hug as the other patrons looked towards us quizzically. The bar, I was sure, had witnessed much more melodrama than two girls, one of them in tears, engaging in a harmless embrace; the attention of the onlookers was only fleeting.

'I have never spoken about this with anyone and the only reason I am telling this to you is that I want you to take a leaf from the experiences I have already endured. After my break-up I too was heart broken and felt as though the world had come to a crumbling end. It was painful and I had no one that I could lean on to. If I was to come out of the depressing state, I had to do it all alone and that is what I did. I pulled up my socks and decided to lead life on my own terms, pledging to myself that I will never land up in a similar vulnerable state ever again.'

'Once I was out of the clutches of love, surprisingly I began to see merit in all that Nirav had said. The world isn't indeed as pious as we sometimes assume it to be and not everything works the way it is meant to. It is all about power and authority and if you were not born with it, you can acquire it by making a few minor concessions with your bourgeois principles, especially if you happen to be a girl. And every time I went about testing my hypothesis, my conviction, that only the end matters and not the means only grew stronger. And I guess, since this is how Nirav thought all along, maybe he had never actually loved me.'

'The idea is not to bore you with my views on life or other such abstractions. The point I am trying to make is that maybe Ravi never loved you or even if he did, he fell out of it. Such things happen. Men are known to be fickle minded, opportunistic and assholes. You can either choose to fret over them and waste your time or you can opt to go on with life on your own terms and face each day as it unfolds.'

She seemed to be making a lot of sense. After all, wasn't that exactly what I was doing, wasting my life by clinging on to a past that was never meant to be eternal? Ravi was gone from my life and if he had to come back, he would have done so already. I was being foolish by reeling under something I could not control while Ravi, the perpetrator of it all, happily went about his life in just the fashion he wanted to.

The discussion with Kamini went a long way in shaping my outlook towards life in the times to come. It wasn't a sudden turning point whereby I underwent an instantaneous metamorphosis but it did lay the foundations for a gradual transformation that saw me changing into someone very different from the Sejal Patel of a few years back.

NINE

'Oh la la... And if I may ask, just where are you heading decked up like that?' Kamini had entered the house just as I was getting out. 'Nice no? It's the same dress we had picked up at Fashion Street. Well worth the money; you should have taken one too,' I replied as she scrutinized the garment. 'It is the corporate event that Sharad Bhai had spoken about; the one that you had turned down,' I added.

They are right when they say that it is all about the mind. The realization that had dawned upon me during the conversation with Kamini had stuck on and I had resolved to mend my ways with immediate effect. I started accompanying Kamini for her parties and outings; drinking, smoking and making the most of what life had to offer. She had a large and diverse set of friends - people from work, common friends of hers and Nirav's who she was still in touch with, friends from the events that she went to and just friends that she couldn't recall where she had met - as a result of which there never seemed to be a dull moment in her life. There always was a party to attend or a set of friends to meet and when that did not happen, the two of us went out on our own, exploring the city in our own blithe manner.

I was amazed at my own adaptability and the eagerness with which I took to life in the fast lane. What had started as a conscious escape from the fortress of solitude I had erected around myself soon became an integral part of my being. Initially I was intrigued and partially amazed at the world Kamini and her friends lived in; one of utter debauchery and tumbling moralities. I was no bastion of morality myself, but still, the one night stands and their social tolerability, uninhibited expression and acknowledgement of ones sexuality, cougars lurking with their honey traps and their oft-eager preys, had been a surprise to begin with. It was amazing how a completely different world coexisted with my own and incredibly enough, had managed to remain hidden from my knowledge.

However, as time passed, I found myself shifting from a phase of curious discoveries and bafflement to one of acceptance and understanding. The new world had welcomed me with open arms and I had uninhibitedly surrendered myself to its bindings. Within a few months I found myself spending more and more time with Kamini and her odd mix of friends, making some of my own along the way. The appeal of their carefree and untroubled existence as well as my urgent need for an emotional detachment with Ravi had attracted me towards them and much before I realized, I was thinking, breathing and living like one of them.

At work too, my damn-to-the-world attitude seemed to be

rubbing off and I was spending only the bare minimum time in office that I could without the risk of losing my job. When I wasn't actually out on calls, I was using them as an excuse to remain out of the premises. Of course I was keen to maintain a safe distance from Ravi as well. And as a constructive engagement for the ample free time that suddenly seemed to have surfaced, I had met Sharad Bhai and given him my resume and some photographs.

Sharad Bhai was one of the quintessential Gutkha-chewing, untucked shirt clad entities who formed the not so glamorous backbone of the fancy parties and dazzling events that were regular features in the city. He was a model coordinator, a fancy title for a man who engaged in supplying manpower to meet any kind of client requirements; some requirements, I suspected, of extremely private nature. Since Kamini had already been working with him, I did not face any difficulties in approaching him and in no time my name too was on his rooster of models, participating in odd exhibitions and events.

It was the annual town-hall for the Maharashtra circle of one of the telecom companies for which Sharad Bhai had approached both Kamini and me. The event was being organized at a banquet hall in one of the city hotels on a Saturday evening and the agenda included the usual speeches by senior management members, recognition for the high performers, followed by dance and drinks. They needed promoters for ushering employees to their seats, handing over plaques and certificates to the dignitaries who in turn would hand them over to the winners, and generally adding a tinge of glamour to the otherwise mundane evening.

Kamini had some prior engagement, a colleague's birthday or something, and she had turned down the offer while at three thousand rupees for just the one evening I was only glad to accept. There was no prescribed dress-code for us promoters and we had been simply asked to dress up formally. Clad in a maroon Lycra dress, heels and a touch of makeup, I was heading for the event when Kamini had intercepted me at the door.

In all there were about a dozen girls waiting outside the banquet hall and as directed by Sharad Bhai, I went ahead and joined them. I was familiar with some of them from past events that we had done together and we were soon exchanging notes on the kind of work each one had lined up ahead, waiting for someone to instruct us on what we needed to do. The wait wasn't long as soon a young, flustered looking man approached, almost jogging up to us.

'You are the promoters?' he asked and without waiting for an answer or offering an introduction, added, 'Come, follow me. Hurry.' We scampered behind him inside the main hall which was a picture of pandemonium and utter chaos. A bunch of people were up on the make-shift stage, converged on a laptop and intermittently staring at the two giant screens that had been erected on either side – some unforeseen technical snag, I presumed. Waiters were scurrying about the hall trying to reinstate order in the arrangement of chairs which were being continuously disturbed by another group of men who were engaged in putting up banners and standees across the hall.

Our escort led us to a man, one who by the looks of things was the person responsible for the proceedings, if not currently in control, and was screaming out to everyone in his vicinity. He was formally dressed with a blazer, tie and the works, and was clearly upset with the pace of the arrangements. 'You guys want me to lose my job Pravin? People will start arriving in about half an hour and even the bloody hall is not ready yet,' he screamed at the man who had ushered us inside before quickly shifting his attention towards the stage. 'Amit, is it done yet? You are not preparing some complex fucking electronic circuit here; all you need to do is connect the bloody laptop to the screens. Is that too much of a rocket science?'

'Almost done sir,' someone yelled back from the stage. 'I have been hearing that for twenty minutes. Get it done right now,' he snapped before turning back towards Pravin. 'I had personally requested you to monitor the preparations Pravin, and this is what greets me barely minutes before the event!' he said, uttering the first low-pitch sentence I heard from him. The man in the jacket was the distraught client, I assumed, and Pravin et al were perhaps from the agency that was handling the event.

'We will be done in time Sir, don't worry! The promoters are here, so if you would want to assign them to their posts,' Pravin replied, gesturing with his hand towards us as we stared on like a bunch of brainless zombies. 'If I had to do all the intellectual masturbation myself, wouldn't I be running an event agency instead of standing here and boiling my blood?' his brief composure was shattered once again and he was back to his screaming ways. But even before Pravin could react, he turned towards us and said, 'Pardon my language, just that we are terribly challenged on time. I am Gaurav Gogia and I work with the Marketing department at WindCel. Now, if each of you could please give me a brief one-line introduction.'

The guy had a way with words and more importantly he hadn't forgotten his chivalry lessons. I was impressed at the swift transition in his mannerism and tone when he addressed us. 'Get the two of them backstage – Neeta and Shilpa, right? Sejal can manage the registration desk and rest of them will remain inside the auditorium to guide guests to their seats,' he addressed Pravin.

I was glad to be picked out from the lot. Whatever meager differentiation there was in our assigned chores, it was a nice feeling to have been singled out from the bunch. The task wasn't particularly complex, I was stationed at the registration desk just outside the hall and all employees walking in were required to sign in a register I was maintaining. I had also been given a bunch of badges that I had to hand over to the attendees once they were done signing the register.

Initially, as the attendees poured in, I was slightly flustered, trying to keep my pace and ensure that the queue ahead of me did not become long enough to be termed as a bottleneck. But once all employees were safely holed up inside the hall, I had all the time at hand. One off attendees continued to trickle in, but once I heard the microphone in the hall come to life and the door was summarily shut, I relaxed. It was odd sitting alone and doing absolutely nothing, so I took out my mobile phone and engrossed myself in a game of Snakes.

'Finally, some time to relax, hmm?' Thankfully the interruption came just when I had completed the seventh stage and was moving on to the eighth. My previous best was five. I looked up from the phone screen to face Gaurav. Now that the event was underway without any evident glitches, he was visibly relaxed and was supporting a smile. 'Yes... Yes Sir,' I mumbled. The smile had done little to erase the image of a screaming man from just a while back and I found myself somewhat scared in his presence.

'Sejal, right?' he continued. I nodded. 'I noticed you handled the registration desk pretty efficiently. Good job done.'

'Thank you sir,' I replied, unable to contain a slight blush from adding to the blusher on my cheeks. 'Gaurav, call me Gaurav. 'Sir' makes me feel old,' he replied, widening his grin. 'So, what do you do?'

'I have a day job with an outdoor media company... space selling. These events are just to keep me occupied outside of work and also help me with some pocket money,' I replied, inadvertently defending my presence at the event despite a full-time employment. He chit-chatted for a few more minutes, asking me the usual questions like where I had come from, which part of the city I stayed in and how was I taking to Mumbai. I had spent nearly three years in the city and yet the question about whether I liked it or not kept creeping up at an alarming regularity. Strange!

'Here, this is my card. I handle events and promotions for my company and often require smart and well-spoken hosts. Tragically most girls coming through these agencies can't even speak a single sentence in English without making it sound like some of the Pakistani cricketers speaking in a post match presentation ceremony, so it will be nice if you could drop me a line with your contact details,' he said, smiling on the joke that I was yet to latch on to, before taking my leave. I surrendered the card into my purse and got back to conquering the next level of Snakes.

I can't exactly tell whether it was my hypersensitive imagination or there was actually some truth to it, but I had noticed a certain change in Ravi's behavior of late. The same desperation to leave office on time and the same exaggerated effort at making a relationship seem cordial that I knew from the early days of our own relationship was once again on display. The facade might have worked for others but since I had seen him engage in exactly the same antics at a time when no action of his escaped my affectionate eyes, it had immediately caught my attention.

The focus of his deliberate ignorance was Tina, a young bubbly girl who had recently joined our team. Disgusting, as I felt towards what was transpiring, I could not deny the fact that Tina had a unique appeal to her: an innocent effervescence coupled with a childish charm that had caught the attention of most men at work. It only made me feel worse.

There was no word about Ravi's engagement or his forthcoming marriage and with the knowledge that he had something going with Tina, I was certain that I had been taken for a ride. I was mad at my naivety for allowing it to happen and I couldn't help notice the flashing glances and knowing smiles the two exchanged ducking the radars of our other colleagues. I was once again spending a lot of time thinking about him, a situation I had mistaken to have become a thing of the past.

If I were to refrain from slipping back into the abyss of my broken heart, I had no option but to get out of there. It was unfair to expect myself to remain indifferent and apathetic while the same saga, of which I had once been an integral part, unfolded in front of my eyes. Whatever little attention I had been channeling towards my work was further dwindling and with each passing day I found my internal turmoil scaling newer levels of mayhem.

I had updated my resume on the job portals some time back and now I was visiting the cyber café on a daily basis to circulate it to potential employers. My efforts were yet to bear fruit when I attended the dreaded weekly review meeting where my worst fears came to life. I didn't have anything substantial to show for the current month or the preceding one and though Ravi had once again blended the two-line update I had given him with that of rest of the team, Promila had singled me out this time around. For the lack of enough artillery for defense, Ravi had glanced at me to supply the justification and this moment of discomfort had been enough to tick her off.

'What the fuck do you guys think you are being paid for? Do you think it is your dad's company and that we are here to pay you your monthly pocket money?' she began in her trademark pitch. She was speaking to no one in particular but it was evident that I was the intended target for her words. I listened to her with my head bowed and my mind working overtime to supply images of Tina smirking at my plight. Her presence in the room made matters worse.

The meeting concluded with a clear warning that unless we were able to log in at least one deal every two months, we had no business being employed with the company and that Promila would personally monitor our individual performances for the current month. I slipped out to the ladies room before the other colleagues could catch me to shower a stream of empathy that I was in no mood to bear.

As I fumbled inside my bag and pulled out a pack of tissues another piece of paper emerged and fell on the floor. The words, 'Gaurav Gogia – Marketing Manager, WindCel Cellular Services' stared back at me as I reached out for it. The card, whose existence I had completely forgotten, had suddenly emerged out of the blue. Maybe it was a sign from the Gods or maybe just a stupid coincidence. But there was no harm in trying, I thought as I pocketed the card.

'Hi Sir, this is Sejal. We had met during your event a few weeks back,' I said when after three rings I heard Gaurav's husky voice on the line. 'Oh… of course, Hi Sejal, how have you been? I thought you had completely forgotten me; and it seems you don't like my name much… still sticking to the 'sir', eh?'

'No sir… I mean, Gaurav. Nothing like that,' I responded, trying to match the familiarity of his tone. We had barely met once and though I am not much into social segmentation, but still, he was a senior employee with a big company and I had merely been a promoter. His overindulgence was slightly surprising, but I played along.

'Actually, I was looking for a change of jobs and was wondering if you would know of some relevant openings within your organization,' without much ado I blurted out the reason that had prompted me to make the call. 'It would be a privilege for any organization to have a dedicated and efficient worker like you on their rolls. If there is no immediate role available, one can be carved out to accommodate you. Why don't we catch up for coffee sometime and discuss this?'

'Sure, whenever you are free,' I replied, obviously elated at the free-flowing compliments. 'How about tomorrow, say 6.30?'

The coffee meeting with Gaurav went off well. He was mildly flirtatious, but which man sipping coffee in the company of a pretty girl isn't? It wasn't anything alarming though and in the midst of general chit-chat we also went on to discuss my aspirations and desired career path. Since Gaurav himself was a marketing professional, I expressed my interest in the same field with the optimism that it would be easier for him to find a role for me within his own team. My only motivation was to get as far away from my current place of employment and from Ravi as I could.

Gaurav proved to be a man of his words and within a fortnight of our discussion I had an offer letter from WindCel in my hands. I had been recruited as a Marketing Executive to handle the coordination with agencies and vendors that Gaurav's team engaged for various activities they undertook.

TEN

WindCel was a stark contrast to my earlier workplace with its swanky office, a sea of employees and inclusive work culture. Though it took me a few days to come to terms with all the names and introductions that had been flung my way, I had a feeling that I was going to enjoy working with my new set of colleagues. There were middle-aged, experienced people and there were the young vivacious ones, most bound together by their illustrious pedigrees. It was a collection of minds emerging from the best institutions of the country and with years and years of unfailing corporate experience and yet none of them carried any unnecessary air about themselves. Each of them seemed eager to extend help and assist those around, much unlike my previous workplace.

Gaurav was a star performed and a blue-eyed boy for Kavita, the Marketing Head for our circle and also Gaurav's boss. Other than me he had three Assistant Managers reporting to him, each handling events, on ground activations and outdoors for an assigned territory. I was to support them centrally; managing the day to day coordination with the vendors they worked with, ensuring timely processing of bills, dispatch and delivery of collaterals and other such support activities.

Gaurav was a tough taskmaster and within my first week I had heard him scream his guts out at all of his other reportees in separate incidents. He instantly reminded me of Promila, but for the fact that he appeared to make an exception when it came to his dealings with me. Maybe because of chivalry, hints of which I had noticed the day I had first met him, or because I was still new to the organization, but invariably he was civil and even charming in his conduct towards me. His cheeky flirtations had not waned since our first coffee meeting and I wasn't exactly complaining.

Another thing that separated him from Promila was that despite the tough demeanor, he commanded unquestionable allegiance and respect from his team members. With the passage of time I realized that this was because Gaurav never screamed at anyone without a logical reason, was understanding and compassionate when it came to rational reasoning and was always there to stand-up for his team members when necessary.

I was glad for everything that my new job brought – significantly higher salary, a better brand to be employed with, a boss I could look up to and far more efficient colleagues. Most importantly, I was glad to have escaped the anguish that had clouded every breathing moment of my life at my previous workplace.

My new job had staked claim to a lion's share of my time and as a result I was compelled to part ways with Sharad Bhai and his troupe. My weekends nevertheless continued to be busy and usually I had a plate-full of parties and outings lined up well in advance. In my tryst to escape my heartburns I had reached out to so many different sets of people that the mere task of keeping up with all of them ended up occupying a better part of my calendar.

One such person I had met during my socializing spree was Vishal Ahuja, originally a friend of Nirav's who had drifted away to becoming Kamini's friend and was now continuing with his drift and steering towards me. He was an aspiring actor with unconventionally good looks, rugged features and a chiseled body. But it was his intelligence and subtle sense of humor that drew me to him the most. I enjoyed his company, just plain platonic conversations and the depth he introduced into them with his wit and knowledge. After the first couple of times we met, we had made it a point to catch-up once every couple of weeks. If there was no party or outing scheduled that would enable us to meet along with rest of the gang, he would simply drop by or call me to one of the nearby joints and we would chit-chat for hours.

He was one of the few people I had called to inform about my job switch. Most of my other newfound friends were either not interested or were incapable of telling the difference between a Marketing and a Sales job. 'Wow, that's fantastic!' he had exclaimed. 'So, Ms Sejal… God! How I hate that name… When do we get our treat?'

'Thanks, but I hope you don't expect me to treat people who don't even like my name?' I teased. 'It is just the name that I can do without, rest of you is pretty enticing I must admit,' he retorted. 'Shut up! And tell me when do you want to meet up? This Saturday works for you?'

We caught up at a local, nondescript bar that served drinks by quarters rather than pegs. 'It's much more economical. And my birthday is approaching, so with the money you save, you can buy me… let's see… how about a Harley Davidson motorbike?' he had dismissed my reservations about treating him there. It turned out to be a good idea after all, since when the fear of a budget-shattering bill is not forcing you to count the drinks, your capacity for alcohol swells dramatically. Soon, we were both slurring incoherently and staring at each other with dilated eyes.

'I need another smoke. You are coming?' I enquired, staggering up from my seat. 'Do I have an option? Who is going to support you if I don't come along? But I don't understand how you all can smoke so much,' he said, getting up to place his hand on my shoulder. Vishal was a non-smoker, not because he was worried about his lungs but because he thought that the smoke was not good for his skin – a fact that I had leveraged on numerous occasions to pull his leg. 'Awww… that's so sweet of you,' I murmured, planting a peck on his cheek.

'You sound so alluring when you are drunk. Sigh… only if I could,' he said once we were in the smoking area and I had succeeded in lighting up my cigarette. 'What could you?' I replied with a naughty grin. Such frivolous flirting was commonplace in our relationship.

'Lots of things. Maybe I would have kissed you for starters,' he said. I could sense a certain tension in the air and he wasn't sounding his usual jovial self. So awkwardly I spoke out the first words that came to me. 'And what is stopping you right now?'

'There are priorities you know, and for me your friendship is much more vital than a few moments of passion. So, if the kiss has any chance of spoiling what we have between us, I am better off without it,' he said with an uncharacteristic seriousness. I was touched. I had met many men by now, indulged them, got pampered by them, but all of them had looked at me as a medium to accomplish their carnal desires. This was the first time that someone had regarded me for what I was, my individuality, and my friendship, and not for the peaks of pleasure I could help them scale.

'Don't look at me as if I am speaking Greek. It is you girls only who end up sullying things with an overdose of emotion,' he said as I continued to stare at him, desperately trying to check my soaring emotions. 'We have made out, so we can't remain friends any longer… blah… blah,' he was now imitating a girl, a heavily accented one at that. Something snapped within me, perhaps the thing that had been holding me back all along, and I reached out and silenced his lips by capping them with mine.

Once the lip-lock ended we hurried back to our table, settled the bill and headed out to his flat. Not a word was spoken in the interim. His flat, if you would term it so, was a one room tenement carved between two floors of a dilapidated building with a partition that separated the toilet cum bath area. There was a single steel cupboard and a bed that was strewn with crumpled garments. But the surroundings didn't matter; the wait had escalated our arousal to desperate levels, blinding us to the surroundings.

As soon as the door shut behind us, we converged on each other like a pack of hungry wolves would on sighting a gullible prey. What followed was intense and unbridled lovemaking, something far more soothing than anything I had ever experienced.

Girls, no matter how pretty they appear to the world, are known to harbor reservations about some part of their anatomy or the other. I too had my own qualms, about my derriere being disproportionately large and the slight deposit of fat on my tummy that I could do without, which when consciously engaging in the act had resulted in my preference for dim or no lighting.

'You know, a higher waist-bum ratio implies higher fertility levels in a girl. It is a natural source of attraction for men… unlike the superficial and cosmetic ones that you girls tend to employ for luring us,' he had said. Vishal had a way of making me comfortable with my own self; I could remain exactly the way I was without forging a mask for the sake of impressing him. We were not lovers, we were friends and that made all the difference.

The next morning, when I got up in his arms, I felt good about life; there was no burden of guilt and no remorse for what had happened, only a glow of satisfaction over a night well spent. Vishal had not engaged in any frivolous banter about being madly in love with me or the likes and yet he had pampered me with admiration and praise, an exchange that left me soaring with an inexplicable sense of freedom and elation.

Unlike the fear Vishal had expressed, our relationship elevated to more mature levels after our little tryst. We remained friends, friends with benefits, as some would have put it. We continued to meet up regularly and every once in a while we made time to cuddle up to each other and relish the moments of raw passion that followed.

There were no commitments, in fact post Ravi I don't think I was even ready for one, and that made our relationship that much more special. I knew about the girlfriends he had been engaging with on the side and the ones that he had been chasing, and I was comfortable speaking with him about any guy that took my fancy. There was affection and care between us and we cherished each other's company, but it was the absence of possessiveness that made our relationship unique and blessed.

We were both aware that our relationship went beyond the barriers of conventionality and that it would be difficult for some of our 'either you are couple or you are not' mindset nurturing friends to digest, so we refrained from bringing what we shared out in open. In a group we continued to behave like the friends we were, keeping our bond a secret from all our common friends, including Kamini. This allowed us to retain our 'single' tags and binge on any interesting opportunity of a fleeting liaison that came our way.

My life had once again taken a turn towards the sunny side. The job was going well and my personal life too seemed to be heading down an unplanned but fascinating path. I was not bound by an affiliation and hence could bask in and occasionally reciprocate to the attention that came my way, of which there was no dearth in my current social framework, and when tired with the exploration and experimenting, I always had Vishal to fall back to.

ELEVEN

'Wow! That's fabulous. I have been meaning to go to Goa for ages now and within six months of joining the job your company is taking you there. Not bad,' was Kamini's reaction to the news. 'Not six, eight long months darling,' I replied, mocking her playfully. We were having a team offsite in Goa. Despite the rave reviews I had heard about the beach-paradise from almost all my friends, I had not managed a visit thus far. It was only a two day jaunt, but I was excited like hell.

'Whatever! But, I will tell you what… You go there are chart out all the happening and must-see places and let's plan a trip of our own once you are back. It will be fun, what say?' she was clearly as excited about the trip as I was.

Over the past eight months I had bonded well with the entire team: Pragati, Namrata and the other girls, the boys, and even Kavita, my super-boss to some extent. My camaraderie with Gaurav had continued on the same footing as it had initially begun – one of mutual respect, some mild flirting and plenty of work. The flirting, I realized, was intrinsic to his nature and he simply could not pass off a chance of making a harmless pass at any girl who would care to listen.

I had slogged hard to learn the nuances of the business, while catering to the work that came my way in the most diligent manner so as to not give him an opportunity to put on display his infamous temper. And he too had responded well, handling me with kid gloves and nurturing me to become a valued resource for the team. I had made a few mistakes, none too glaring though, but he had steered me past them without losing his cool, a fact that I thanked my stars for, since I had no idea as to how I would react if my boss cum friend came down upon me half as heavily as I had often seen him do with others.

WindCel was surely not a thrifty organization and when it came to pampering their employees, there was no stone left unturned. The two-day offsite included just one session of presentations on the Marketing plans for the next year, which too I had learnt to be a known farce to meet the auditory requirements. It was essentially a getaway for the team, allowing them to bond with each other and to have a good time at the company's expense.

The thirty-odd member team was to put up at a Taj property, an expensive affair, I knew, since I had been directly responsible for finalizing all the bookings. We were to leave from Mumbai on Friday evening and return by the Sunday afternoon flight. A formal dinner had been organized for Friday night and early on Saturday we had the mandatory presentation session, leaving the rest of the day free for us to do what we chose. At night we had to assemble in the hotel ballroom where arrangements for drinks and dinner had been made, a casual affair with a makeshift dance floor and a DJ.

Once the presentation session was over, I was faced with a tricky choice: whether to venture out and explore the place I had heard so much about or to stay back and enjoy the awesome hospitality and ambience of the resort. The resort was spread over a sprawling landscape overlooking the Arabian Sea and among other amenities boasted of a state of the art spa, a poolside bar and a coffee shop that had its platform virtually extending into the waters. The temptations were telling, but I was aided in my decision with the unexpected invite from Gaurav.

'We are planning to go out for some shopping to the town and then perhaps a stopover at the Calangute Beach. You want to come along?' He had booked a car from the hotel and our immediate team, Gaurav and his other reportees, were all heading out to the city. Obviously I tagged along, and I was glad I did.

September was at its fag end and the weather was as agreeable as one could hope for. The humid summer heat was way off its peak and a light breeze was adding a flavor of exquisiteness to everything around. The tourist season was just around the corner, I was told, but I could already see faces of assorted origin zipping past on rented motorbikes or wandering about aimlessly, lending an air of tranquil lethargy to the surroundings.

The drive to Panjim, the shopping – unbelievably inexpensive liquor and cashews, the local food – prawns and Goan fish curry, the architecture, the drive to back to the famous Calangute beach and the beach itself, all seemed like a surreal experience unfolding an act at a time. I was instantly in love with Goa and by the visible reluctance of others to return to the hotel, I could gauge that their state wasn't very different.

We returned to the resort with barely enough time for a quick change before we had to assemble in the ballroom. I slipped into the off-shoulder blue dress, the one I had packed especially for the occasion and an easy one to put on, and rushed to the designated hall, arriving just in time to catch Kavita's opening address.

As is customary in most official dos, even an evening of fun and frolic had to be preceded by gratuitous sermons from the higher-ups. Thankfully Kavita was attuned to the mood of the assemblage and limiting her discourse to a few mandatory sentences, she flagged open the bar, officially handing over charge for the evening to the DJ.

Despite the peppy and inviting Bollywood numbers, a large section of the group started with the usual 'warming up to the boss' routine and I could even hear snippets of business-talk, wrestling with the blaring music to be heard, within the little groups that had drifted away to various corners of the hall. But once the drinks began their telling, the homogeneity was established once again and the barriers of rank and designation were quickly drained out. As some colleagues literally dragged a reluctant Kavita to the dance floor, it instantly became the nerve center of the party and every breathing soul, willing or unwilling, was soon stomping away to the DJ's tunes.

I had an awesome time. I couldn't remember the last time I had danced so much and in such an unrestrained manner. Whenever I stepped away from the floor to catch my breath or refill my glass, someone or the other emerged to haul me right back. It was my second or maybe the third drink after which I even got rid of my troublesome heels to return to the floor barefooted, consumed by a renewed vengeance. I wasn't dancing with anyone in particular; it was one of those mad senseless sessions that happen when everyone on the dance floor knows everyone else – human chains, one-on-one aping binges and generally shaking a hip with anyone you bump into – an extravaganza of rampant frolic.

The party went on till Satya, one of our colleagues, having made most of the free booze, began to throw up in the hall itself. There were others, I could tell, who had long busted their limits and were sneaking out to the rest rooms every once in a while, but the mess that Satya created was a completely different order. The music stopped, the lights came on and the party came to an abrupt halt as some of the guys lugged the culprit to the safety of his room and we were compelled to return to ours.

It was well over three by the time we got back and within a matter of minutes, Raupali, the girl I was sharing my room with, was buzzing her way into the folds of sleep. I was still wide awake, distracted by Raupali's incessant snoring or perhaps by contentment from the blissful day gone by. After struggling on the bed for some time I picked up my pack of cigarettes and got out of the room once again.

The resort was unusually quiet and lights in almost all the cottages were out by now. Aimlessly I started strolling down the cobbled path that led to the swimming pool. It was as though the silence was trying to speak to me – arbitrary creaking of crickets, rhythm of my own steps, ruffling of leaves, crashing of waves and the deep, hollow sound of the sea - all converging into a language I was struggling to understand.

I didn't even realize when I left my original path to cut through the garden and surface at its far end, from where I had an unobstructed view of the boundless expanse of water. The tide must have been high, as I could see the waves rolling over the sand and reaching right up to the resort's boundary. The resort had been built on an elevated stretch of land, and in the railing ahead of me I could see a waist-high gate from where one had to descend barely three or four steps to emerge on the small private beach which was now submerged. The gate was locked, but it wasn't much of an obstacle. I did contemplate climbing over it but lethargy prevailed and instead I settled for one of the nearby benches where I could sit and gaze at the sea in peace.

The lighting in the garden was minimal; possibly the resort management wasn't expecting one of its guests to be there at this hour. The soothing white light of the moon and its simmering reflections from the water, though illuminating enough, lent a degree of sublimity and mystique to the entire scenery. I was spellbound. I eased myself on to the bench and lit my cigarette, permitting the alcohol in my system to sway my thoughts from one degree of profundity to another.

I thought about the ethereal stories of love and romance – Romeo and Juliet, Heer and Ranjha – perhaps a calling of the ambience surrounding me, but soon slipped down to other worldly engagements. I think it was the contrast between aggressive mating habits and the perceptible timidity of rabbits that I was musing about, trying to recall if I had ever witnessed rabbits copulating, when the sudden intrusion left me startled.

'Lovely, isn't it?' I heard a voice from not too far behind. My heart skipped a beat as I was instantly dragged back into reality. Within a flash, at least a dozen permutations of who the intruder could be and what all afflictions he could subject me to raced though my head. I turned around to face a familiar figure, recognition slightly delayed due to the unfavorable lighting and heaved a sigh of relief when I realized that it was only Gaurav.

'Phew, you scared the shit out of me,' I said. 'Sincere apologies,' he chuckled, 'I didn't mean to scare you. I wasn't feeling sleepy, so I came to the garden for a stroll and when I saw someone sitting here, I decided to check who it was. Mind if I join?'

He was wearing a T-shirt and Bermudas, his night clothes I guessed, but oddly the musky fragrance of his cologne was still fresh. 'Would he be as aggressive as rabbits?' I couldn't help thinking as he parked himself next to me. I smirked at my own joke; he had caught me at a wrong time and certainly in the wrong frame of mind.

'So, what brings you here?' he asked. 'Nothing. Couldn't sleep, so I thought I might as well soak in as much of Goa as I can while I am here,' I replied, suppressing a giggle. I was now imagining him mounting a fluffy white rabbit, bloated up to his size; or maybe it was he who had shrunk, it didn't matter. The chit-chat didn't last long and soon I felt his hands on my shoulders and his lips reaching out for mine.

Gaurav wasn't particularly good looking but his personality did have a definite charming tinge about it, the in-control, authoritative, successful man that most girls long for. I knew he was married, but even that was inconsequential as a marital alliance was the last thing on my mind in the given circumstances. Though lately my parents had started hounding me in this regard, I had summarily dismissed their pleas, attributing them to their ignorance about life beyond the frontiers of Rajkot. Anyways, his touch was distraction enough for my thoughts to cease their wandering and when his lips met mine, I felt a volcano erupt within me. I was overcome by an unrivalled bout of passion and soon I was literally on top of him, meeting every advance he made with matching intensity.

'My room is just across the garden,' he whispered midst labored breaths and we reluctantly detangled, only to pounce upon each other as soon as we were in the confines of the room. Since I had handled the bookings, I knew that the Managers had single rooms, permitting us all the privacy we needed at the time. It was only with the break of dawn that I sneaked out of his room, spent but satisfied, and sneaked into my own bed beside Raupali. She was still snoring, only a little erratically now.

Gaurav hadn't turned out to be a rabbit, but was perilously close. He had lasted the entire hour with two shuddering orgasms without much ado and had it not been for the need to end our exploits before our colleagues started coming back to life, he seemed to be geared up for more.

I was dragged out of the bed by Raupali, with barely enough time to pack my bag and board the bus that was to ferry us to the airport. I slept through most of the flight and even as I reached home, I was hopelessly tired and ready to hit the bed.

'Babes!' Kamini exclaimed as she opened the door and hugged me excitedly. 'Barely two days and you have a tan already; you must have had a blast, how was it?'

'Welcome back Ms Highflier,' I was greeted by another voice as I stepped inside the house. It was Vishal and he had a glass in his hand, Rum and Coke, his usual drink. There was another half-filled glass on the table which Kamini was now reaching out for. 'So, how was the trip?' he added.

'Great to see you, but how come you are here?' I said to him. In all honesty, this one time I wasn't particularly thrilled to see him. I was tired and in desperate need to hit the bed. The last thing I wanted to do was present an elaborate account of my trip or to have one more alcoholic drink. My head was still heavy from the last set of drinks I had guzzled.

'I was waiting for you. Since you forgot to even wish me on my birthday, I thought it must have been a fantastic trip and that I must get a firsthand download.' He was still smiling but the sarcasm in his voice was more than apparent.

'Fish... Fish... How could I?' I banged my fist on my already throbbing forehead. His birthday was on Saturday and I had remembered it all along except for the day I needed to act on it. I hadn't even called to wish him and that was inexcusable. He had every right to feel bad. I would have felt worse had he done anything similar for my birthday.

'I am so sorry. Wish you a happy belated birthday and an awesome year ahead,' I said, getting up to hug him. 'And I promise to make up to you for it. Come, lets all go out for dinner. My treat,' I added. The fatigue that was refusing to let go was crushed under the burden of guilt and I was keen to make amends for my oversight.

'Thanks! And it is ok; you don't need to be apologetic. We realized we could have a nice time in your absence as well. No?' he said with a smile, adding the question for Kamini to supplement with her affirmation. I knew he was hurt and that he had opted to tease me since he couldn't be more expressive in Kamini's presence. The burden of my guilt only increased and for a fleeting instance I wished Kamini wasn't there so that I could tell him how terrible I was feeling.

After a bit of coaxing Vishal accepted my dinner invite and we headed out to one of the plush restaurants on the road leading up to the Juhu beach. Kamini had not joined us, citing an early morning meeting and the fact that she had already had her dinner as excuses. I got a faint feeling that she wasn't completely oblivious to the supposedly secret liaison transpiring between Vishal and me. I did insist on her coming along, but only lackadaisically and in the end was happy to concede to her wishes.

'You didn't even tell me that you were traveling to Goa,' he said with the first few sips from his wine glass. It wasn't as though he was whining; it was a factual statement spoken in all sincerity. 'I am truly sorry. It happened so suddenly that in all the excitement I forgot to mention it. No justifications, but…,' I reached out for his hands and looked into his eyes. He seemed to understand. 'So, how did you celebrate?' I asked, meaning to dilute some of the weightiness that had seeped into the air.

'Oh well, I thought you would be home, so after finishing some work I had at the dubbing studio, I came straight down to see you. But through Kamini I learnt that you were out of town. My disappointment might have shown since she relentlessly went about probing as to what I wanted to see you about. I told her that it was my birthday and I had hoped to celebrate it with you guys. Nice girl she is... She cancelled her own plans for the evening, ordered a cake, some food, and we stayed back home and chit-chatted along. A nice quiet birthday, not the kind I was hoping for, but a pleasant evening nevertheless.'

'I missed you,' he added, his eyes once again vouching for the sincerity behind the statement. 'Well, I do regret not being there on your special day, but I hope you understand.'

For the first time I felt something concrete, something real, in the vagueness and ambiguity that surrounded our relationship. We sat there for a long time, talking and listening to each other and enjoying even the poignant moments that were emerging between us at an alarming frequency. We spoke about my trip, minus of course the details of my inviolable tryst, and he showed me the tattoo he had got inked on his bicep as a birthday gift for himself. The wound was still raw but in the abrasions I could clearly see the form of a snake wrapped around a vertical sword. Not the kind of design I would have opted for, but with the background of his shapely biceps, I must admit, the tattoo more than justified its worth.

When I returned home I was too exhausted to brood over the evening or the developments of the past few days. But despite my best efforts I could not shake off an uneasy feeling that something important, something that would play a pivotal role in shaping the next chapter of my life, had passed by undetected.

TWELVE

I hadn't come face to face with Gaurav on the day we left Goa and later, once the usual rigmarole of the office resumed, I got a distinct feeling that he was deliberately avoiding me. His usual chirpy greetings and comments had ceased and our interactions had been reduced only to perfunctory bits of conversation. But I wasn't perturbed, in fact I completely understood his stance and at some level I was even glad at his approach.

What had happened between us was more circumstantial than anything and I didn't want him to be clinging on to it or to me for that matter. I was not sure how I would have reacted had he decided to confront me or embarked upon an endeavor to find some deeper meaning beneath the incident. It is so often that men, misguided by the erroneous perception that sex for women can only be an aftermath of some deep rooted emotion, inadvertently tend to exhibit signs of possessiveness or affection. I was relieved that Gaurav hadn't turned out that way.

Moreover I was somewhat distracted by the developments in my personal life to pay much heed to Gaurav or his ploy of ignorance. Though nothing precise or exact had been voiced by either of us, the dinner on the day of my return from Goa had noticeably transformed my relationship with Vishal. While I found myself looking forward to our next meeting, blending my solitude with conjured images of the time we would spend together, for his part he had started seeking my company much more fervently.

Some evenings he would call me, explaining his presence in the vicinity of my office by virtue of some work or meeting, and we would travel back together. When he didn't call, he would drop by and we would share a couple of drinks at home or sneak out for a quick bite. Depending on Kamini's absence from the flat or with a quick visit to Vishal's pad, we had continued engaging in our bouts of passion, only at much regular intervals now.

I had a feeling that our relationship was heading towards its summit and I knew that he thought the same, just that we were both weary of voicing it out aloud for the fear of creating a fissure in the cherished relationship we already shared. Amid all the confusion our friendship had managed to retain its flavor and I could not help but feel fortunate about the regal treatment that life was dishing out to me – a good job, a pleasured existence and hopefully a desirable partner - what else could I hope for? Only, I had forgotten that it is but the core of good fortune where misfortune dwells and I didn't have to wait long for it to surface in its frightful regalia.

It was just a matter of time before I was compelled to take note of Gaurav's revised disposition towards me. I had misspelt a vendor's name – Conflence as against Confluence, in a payment request I had sent to the Finance department. The dimwits in Finance hadn't bothered to verify the name with their own records and had simply issued the cheque as per the name mentioned in my mail. The vendor, unable to bank the instrument, had returned it to our office and the same had somehow landed up on Gaurav's desk.

He had called me on my extension and asked me to see him in his cubicle, a definite deviation from his earlier method of walking up to my desk if and when he needed to talk about something. 'What is this?' he enquired in a stern tone, pushing the cheque on his table towards me.

The error was too insignificant and once again went undetected by the quick glance I shot towards the piece of paper. 'It is the cheque for the payment due to Confluence against the last event,' I artlessly replied, still trying to figure out the reason for being summoned by him. Obviously he didn't need me to tell him what a cheque looked like.

'You don't see anything wrong with it?' his expressions remained firm and his eyes fixated on mine. Still baffled, I picked up the cheque to scrutinize it closely and that was when I became aware of the spelling error. 'Oh, the name has been misspelt,' I muttered. 'I am glad you noticed. I checked with Finance and they claim that this was how you had spelt the name in your request.'

'I don't think the mistake was in my request mail,' I said, following my natural instinct for denial, before adding, 'Anyhow, I will get it corrected immediately and dispatch the revised cheque to the vendor today itself.'

'It is all so simple isn't it?' his voice was reeking with sarcasm. 'Why can't you do such a simple thing right? If I need to sit here and spell-check every mail you send out, what is the point of having you here at all? It will be much simpler for me to send out the mails myself,' he was now screaming out aloud, just like I had seen him do on numerous occasions. Only this time I was the target.

'Gaurav, it is a simple typing error which could happen with anyone. I am not even sure if the mistake was in my mail, I can check that and confirm to you. This is the first time that such a thing has happened and I am saying that I will get it corrected immediately,' I tried to reason, but he clearly was in no mood to listen.

'So, are you saying that the folks in Finance are lying? First you make a mistake and then you have the bloody nerve to stand here and argue with me,' I could see anger welling up in his eyes, only I didn't know if the magnitude of his reaction was justified. There was no point in carrying on with the debate; it wasn't likely to reach a conclusion, so I listened in silence as he continued with his reprimand, eventually dismissing me with instructions to 'immediately' rectify my mistake.

I was feeling terrible when I returned to my seat; it never is a great feeling to have been admonished publicly, especially when its basis and legitimacy remains questionable. I had witnessed his outbursts before, but usually they had been within the periphery of logic and reasoning. So, for the sake of my bruised esteem, I decided to give him the benefit of doubt. There wasn't much else I could think of doing anyways. 'He is a guy so it can't possibly be PMS. Maybe an early morning quarrel with the wife or just a bad day in general,' I told myself.

The comfort that the self-pacification provided also turned out to be momentary as his conduct towards me only became harsher there on. It was as though the guise of civility had suddenly been washed off his being and having once seized the chance to exhibit his true colors, he had developed some perverse liking for it. He began to snap at me with disturbing regularity, irrespective of whether an opportunity was indeed present or needed to be conjured, making my work life a saga of agony and torment.

The sudden change in Gaurav's demeanor did not go unnoticed and some concerned colleagues did inquire about the underlying reason, but I could only shrug helplessly. I was as clueless as they were. And that was not the only worry to have made a sudden appearance in my otherwise content life. My parents had taken their tenacious resolve to get me married to disconcerting levels of lunacy.

The culprit, I later learnt, was some bogus Tantrik they had consulted who had poisoned them with the idea that if I didn't get married within the next six months, I would remain a spinster for the rest of my wretched life. This had prompted them to take on the mantle of liberating me from the curse of my stars upon themselves and they had intensified their efforts to materialize a suitable match for me. When I had objected, bargaining for some more time, my father had served me with an ultimatum to visit home within the next fortnight if I wished to have a say in choosing my own life partner, failing which, he would do the honors and come down to invite me for my own wedding.

The tensions I was plagued with had begun to show on both my face and my conduct and both Kamini and Vishal had taken note, making several attempts to make me talk and share my burden. Since I didn't want to sound as though it was an effort to make him commit to me, I chose Kamini over Vishal. Moreover, I wasn't feeling comfortable about sharing the entire chronology of events that had blemished my relationship with Gaurav with the man I think I was falling in love with.

'Why don't you tell them about Vishal? That should take care of their concerns,' she said in response to my pre-nuptial woes. 'Vishal! What about Vishal?' I exclaimed.

'Babes, I know you from the time you roamed about in your bloomers,' she responded with a knowing smirk. 'You think I cannot see? He loves you, you love him and he is a nice guy – good looking, from a decent family and all of that. So, why wouldn't you want to tell your folks about him?'

She knew me too well; there was no point beating around the bush with her. 'Ya, I do like him… but the problem is that I haven't told that to him as yet, and for that matter, neither has he. Besides, he is still struggling to make something out of his acting career. How do you suppose I could go about asking him to marry me?' I said.

'If you haven't told him about your feelings, well, you must. And as for the decision about marriage, you can always share your predicament and leave him to make the decision,' she retorted. She was right in a very detached sort of a way; she wasn't aware of the niceties of my relationship with Vishal and there was no way that I could explain them to her. I couldn't explain to her that I would rather face the music alone than to burden him with the load of commitment at this point in his career. We were friends and I needed to support him instead of using him to alleviate my own troubles.

So I opted to switch the discussion to the other pressing concern that was plaguing me, quietly resolving to visit home soon and make myself heard in person. I had a feeling that my parents, especially my father, would be more sympathetic towards my cause if I were to present my case in flesh and blood.

Kamini listened intently, as I narrated everything from the first time I met Gaurav, our Goa escapade and the sudden transition in his behavior thereafter. 'So, what's so surprising about it?' she said after a thoughtful pause. Surprisingly her voice betrayed not an iota of angst or fury and instead was laced with an eloquent calmness. 'Meaning?' I sought a more comprehensive explanation.

'He saw you - a pretty, attractive girl - and would have been possessed by the desire to take you to bed. Just like it happens with all the men. He fawned over and wooed you so that you would give in and once his purpose was achieved, he went back to being his usual self. Every man houses two distinct personalities within him: one, when his actions are governed solely by the surge of testosterone and the other when he is actually using his brains to think. In this case you barely happened to witness both sides of Gaurav within a very short span of time. That's about all there is to it.'

'But that doesn't entitle him to start treating me like a lump of shit, does it? I mean, I am ok if he wishes to detach himself from me or something, but he can't transcend the barriers of civility just because we have slept together, can he?' I interjected.

'Sweetheart, he can do that, and as a matter of fact that's exactly what I understand he has been doing. No? Maybe he was always a loud and uncouth person and it was you who missed noticing it, maybe it is some sort of a guilt pang he is trying to overcome, or he simply could be deriving some perverse pleasure by showing you who is in charge – putting you in your rightful place, so to say. Whichever the case may be the fact remains that he is in a position of power and whether to your liking or not, he is using it as he pleases.'

I had always regarded Kamini for her understanding of the way a male mind works, but today she seemed to be speaking in a language different from the one I wanted to hear. I knew that Gaurav, being my boss, exerted a certain degree of influence over me and that he was using all of it to make my life miserable. Her reasoning, though not completely convincing, did give me multiple theories to choose from to explain the sudden shift in his behavior. But I still didn't know what I could or should be doing to emerge from the quandary.

'So, do you mean I should keep my head bowed and accept all that he decides to fling towards me? I work for the company and not for him. I am not his personal slave and he my master that I need to accept his trashy conduct,' I almost screamed out of frustration.

'No, that is not what I am suggesting. As I see it, you have two options to choose from; you can either have a one-on-one chat with him to try and sort things out or instead you could decide to stand up to him. I am not sure if the first option will work, it might just give some unwarranted boost to his ego and give him the impression that his ploy is working exactly the way he wanted it to. This might make him all the more adamant on pursuing his current line of action. The second option, on the other hand, is risky and will have to be well thought through,' she was almost mumbling to herself now. After another pause she added, 'Give me some time to think. It is a tricky situation and we must not act in haste.'

Our conversation was cut short by a call from my parents. Gaurav and his antics momentarily evaporated from my mind as I valiantly tried to hold my ground against the badgering that both of them were alternatively subjecting me to. By the time the call ended, I was stiff tired and I had committed to them that I would visit home over the coming weekend. It was Wednesday already.

Later, when I retired to the bed, I relayed the entire conversation with Kamini once again in my head, still unable to make head or tail of it. I was feeling used, rather used and discarded, like the treatment we so often met out to hand-wipes and paper tissues. It was a loathsome feeling. Eventually I dozed off, swimming between sinewy emotions of disgust, repugnance and extreme exasperation.

THIRTEEN

'Can you come here please?' it was Gaurav on the line and once again I had been summoned in a somewhat ominous fashion. I tried to think hard for any thing I had done to warrant a reprimand, as I walked up to his seat. I couldn't think of any.

'What do you think, this is a guest house or something?' he started in his familiar pitch. I stood looking at him, hoping to be enlightened about my misdeed so that I could offer a counter. 'You can't just apply for a leave at such short notice and expect me to approve it. When and who do you intend to hand over your pending tasks to? And don't you think you should have discussed it with me before putting the leave request on the system?'

The reason for his eruption was the two day leave I had applied for just a while back. Since I was anyways going home, I had planned to spend two extra days there and return on Tuesday night. I had a day and half to go in the office and I was hoping to finish my pending jobs before boarding the bus on Friday evening. I was a mere Executive and my absence, such a brief one at that, was surely not going to hamper the organization's regular functioning.

As for not having a discussion with him before applying for the leave on the system, I hadn't heard of that being the standard practice. The system gave the line manager the liberty to approve, reject or reschedule the leaves and if a verbal approval had to be obtained before the online application, what was the purpose of the online system in the first place?

It clearly was another one of Gaurav's petty excuses for screaming at me and I could suddenly feel a tendon distend in my temple. '… putting you in your rightful place… showing you who is in charge…,' Kamini's words rang through my ears and I felt sick in my stomach. I was simmering with rage and my jaws were clenched so hard that a few of my molars could easily have popped out. I took a deep breath and another and yet another before I found myself able to articulate my response.

'Something urgent came up for which I need to visit my hometown. It is just a two day leave and I will complete all my work between today and tomorrow,' I said. Though he was looking straight at me, I wasn't sure if he was listening to even a word of what I said. 'Stop staring at me like that. Who do you think you are?' he screamed once again.

Without a thought I turned around and started walking back to my seat. He shouted my name a couple of times, but I didn't even care to look back. I had had enough of his bullying. I was no longer going to be the sacrificial goat for him to derive his sadistic kicks and ego stimulations from. He had no right to treat me like a piece of trash and if there was a time that I had to stand up to him, it was now. My eyes had turned moist even while I stood facing him and now tears were gushing out of them profusely.

I got up, using my handkerchief to wipe the dampness off my cheeks, strategically leaving a few residual drops lurking about my eyelids and headed towards Kavita's cabin. 'What happened to you?' she exclaimed, getting up from her seat, understandably taken aback by the image I presented. 'I need to speak with you,' I let the words slip out hesitantly. 'Of course. Have a seat. You need some water?'

After some encouragement from her I went on to apprise her about my situation with Gaurav, not a completely candid version but not very far from the truth either. I told her that he had been behaving flirtatiously, passing playful remarks from the day I stepped into office, a fact not hidden from many and compounded by the perception he enjoyed. I didn't have to spend much time in establishing the rapport I had initially shared with Gaurav and quickly I moved on to narrating the incident from Goa.

'It was after the party ended, the day before we had to leave. I wasn't feeling sleepy so I stepped out into the garden and in some time Gaurav too turned up and sat beside me. I was slightly drunk and didn't take any particular notice when he started stroking my hair. But when he started massaging my shoulders, I instinctively withdrew and told him to stop since it was making me feel uncomfortable. He stopped, but only momentarily. He began telling me about how I needed to remain in the good books of my superiors if I was to make a career for myself within the organization and as he did so, his hands once again started stroking my hair.'

I hadn't practiced it and yet a twisted version of the episode was flowing from me as freely as any truth I had known. Perhaps it was my natural instinct to project an unsullied self-image which had taken on the role of an editor, and unprepared as I was, I let my conscious remain a bemused spectator to the picture that my words were painting.

'And then he suddenly kissed me. I was too startled to react. I didn't know what to do; I hadn't in my wildest dreams expected him to come on to me like this. Harmless flirtations are one thing and this, completely another. I was stunned, fighting the alcohol induced haze to arrive at the appropriate response, while he continued kissing and fondling me.'

By now I had Kavita's undivided attention. She was looking at me expectedly as though waiting for the next twist in her favorite television soap to unfold, I obliged. 'When I couldn't take it any more, I pushed him aside and sternly asked him to stop. I told him that I respected him as a senior, as a boss, and that I wasn't interested in having anything to do with him beyond that. He was suddenly hit by a wave of remorse and started apologizing, blaming the alcohol for his deplorable behavior. He said that his room was close by and we should go there and talk things out instead of discussing them in the open. 'Someone might hear us,' he said. I told him that there was no need for a discussion and that I would not hold anything against him. But he was insistent and said that he wouldn't be able to sleep in peace after what he had done. He kept pleading for me to allow him to express his apologies for the sake of his sanity, till, for the lack of any alternatives, I agreed.'

'Once in the room, it took little time for him to come back to his depraved, corrupt self. He pounced on me and... and... I wanted to scream, but I was scared; if someone discovered us in that situation, obviously I would have been blamed for being present in his room at that hour. I didn't know what to do. My parents, they would have died...,' I left the words tailing and burst into an incessant sob. Kavita rushed to console me.

'Control, control yourself Sejal. You need to be strong,' she said, handing me a glass of water from her desk. By now the line between reality and illusion had blurred beyond identification. I had reached a stage where I myself was no longer sure of which among the two accounts was the truth: the happenings from that night as I vaguely remembered them or the reconstruction that my words were now shaping. I was sailing with the part of the hapless, wronged, victim that I had assigned to myself and the suitable motifs were materializing effortlessly. She continued with her comforting words till I was ready to resume again.

'I tried to think of it as a terrible nightmare and attempted to brush it aside, limiting my interactions with Gaurav to the bare minimum. But clearly he had other ideas. He asked me out again and when I curtly declined, he threatened me with dire consequences,' I said and went on to describe in detail the inflictions that he had been subjecting me to, right up to the recent spat pertaining to my leave application. 'I know even I am at fault. I shouldn't have let such a thing happen in the first place and God knows that I tried to live with the guilt to the extent that I could. But now it has become unbearable. I can't come into office every day, fearing the pretext he would use to humiliate me next. I am sorry for burdening you with this, but I just couldn't take it any more...'

I didn't know whether what I had done was right or wrong and I was clueless as to what the repercussions of my actions would be, but I wasn't perturbed by the least bit. Gaurav had pushed me to a corner where I was left sullied and violated for no fault of mine. I had to hit back, if not for the sake of revenge then for the sake of my esteem, and that was exactly what I had done.

'Sejal, you did the right thing. It was extremely brave of you to bring it out in the open. Being a woman, I understand the kind of courage this would have required. I am sorry for all that you had to undergo and rest assured I shall leave no stone unturned to ensure that justice is delivered. I will have a word with HR and figure out the way forward, meanwhile you try and get a grip on yourself,' she said, holding and patting my hand in a reassuring gesture. 'And why don't you take the day off tomorrow as well? You can return to office on Wednesday straightaway; the time off should do you some good,' she added.

'What time are you planning to leave office?' it was a text message from Vishal. Since I had emerged from Kavita's room, I had spent some time locked up in the ladies room reasoning with myself about my actions. My allegations weren't unprecedented; there were hundreds of stories, confirmed and unconfirmed, about sexual exploits facilitated by command, power and hierarchy of the corporate world that one comes across on a regular basis. And if the past examples were any indication, it was often the victim (a female, in all the cases I could recall) who got the benefits of sympathy and consideration. Why would my case be any different? After all, there were no witnesses that night and it would only be his word against mine.

Partly convinced, I had returned to my desk and engaged myself in sending out necessary mails preceding my brief absence. Just once I had caught a fleeting glance of Gaurav and I had immediately turned the other way. I was feeling relieved, as though a heavy burden had alighted from my back, and also a mean and wicked pleasure over what lay in store for my tormentor. Though unplanned, I was proud of myself for having contrived a just rejoinder for Gaurav. 'Another 15 minutes of so, why?' I replied.

'Great, buzz me when done. I am around, will pick you up,' the reply came within a matter of minutes.

It is amazing how even a slight rupture in the façade of ones worries sends a wave of relief gushing in and I was glad to have Vishal for company in my moment of liberation. I gladly took him up on the suggestion for a quick cup of coffee before heading home and soon we were sitting across the table at a nearby coffee shop.

'I hear you are planning a visit home?' he asked casually. This should have sent my systemic alarms in motion since I hadn't told anyone but Kamini about my plans yet, but I was too oblivious to bother.

'Yes, leaving tomorrow and should be back by Tuesday,' I heedlessly replied.

'Any specific reasons for the sudden plan?' he continued. 'Nothing much, generally,' I shrugged. As I looked for more convenient topics to steer the conversation towards, a discomfiting silence ensued on the table which was eventually broken by Vishal.

'There is something I have been meaning to tell you for a while now, but it was only today after I spoke with Kamini that I could muster enough courage to do so,' he said, letting his right hand slip into his trouser pocket. 'Not the most romantic of proposals, but Sejal, will you be mine?' he said, handing me a small velvet box. He hadn't opened the box for me and neither had he made the effort to get down on his knees, but that moment remains etched in my memory till date.

It was as unadulterated, as honest a moment as there could be. The ring was simple; a band of gold sans any gems or precious stones, but I could tell that the fit was perfect. I couldn't claim to not have thought about Vishal as a prospective life partner, especially after my discussions with Kamini, but this was much beyond my expectations.

He had his fair share of pros and cons – while he was hardworking and ambitious, his choice of profession was plagued with uncertainties, he was pleasing to the eye and had a charming persona, but his qualifications left plenty to be desired, he came from a decent family, but he had surrendered all his interests and set off alone to carve a career in acting against their better judgment. But the choice for me was only obvious and the one thing responsible for tilting the scales in his favor was the marvelous relationship we shared.

I knew that if there was one person I could lead an unrestrained life with, it was Vishal. In him I saw a life of joy and jubilance, not shackled by the constraints of an orthodox marriage and a promise of undemanding tutelage that could only result from the firm foundations of friendship.

I had evaluated his candidature within the confines of my solitude and he had emerged with flying colors. Only I wasn't expecting to be confronted with the need to voice the results so soon. I was baffled, elated and nervous at the same time, a feeling that left me grappling for words as I sat staring at the little velvet box in my hand. Both Vishal and I knew the eventual outcome of the proposal and perhaps the simplest thing for me would have been to utter a simple yes. 'Oh, you sure know how to spring a surprise, don't you? You are a great friend, an amazing person, someone I love being with, but marriage is another thing altogether. I need some time to think. Hope you understand?' I heard myself saying instead.

'Fair enough, but do me a favor and keep this with you for now. You can always return it if you end up deciding otherwise,' he said, handing back the little box that I had involuntarily pushed towards his half of the table. 'If I keep it with me, I might just be tempted to try it on some other willing finger as well. You never know,' he added with a wink.

In his trademark style he had once again deprived a serious matter of all its gravity and left it to float in the domain of frivolousness, but the look of sedulous affection in his eyes was unmistakable. Life for him was always a tranquil, easy-paced walk in the park and there was nothing that seemed to have the wherewithal to perturb him.

We left the coffee shop, my conviction only strengthened that if there was any one person I could imagine spending the rest of my life with, it was Vishal.

FOURTEEN

I boarded the bus back to Mumbai on Monday evening, a day sooner than originally planned. At the helm of my hasty retreat was the benevolence wrapped coercion my parents had resorted to, but that was not it. Everything about my hometown seemed to have undergone a transition since I had last visited. The streets seemed narrower and dustier with a look of endless lethargy about them, the people walking them seemed nonchalant, somewhat brusque and I found myself wanting to place them in the fondness of my earlier memories.

I knew I had started on the wrong footing when my mother voiced a diffident objection to the garment I had pulled out of my bag to change into. It was only a tank top for Christ's sake! I failed to understand how an entire town, sadly, of which my parents were still a part, could have a selective vision about changes that were shaping around them. While a girl wearing a backless Choli was completely acceptable, she would be frowned upon when wearing a simple tank top. Girls zipping about on their two-wheelers were in conformity but all hell would break loose if one of them decided to ride pillion behind a guy. The contrivance of a town that had once been my own now seemed alien, or perhaps it was I who had chosen to alienate myself instead.

I junked the tank top and settled for a t-shirt instead; I had a long battle ahead and it was in my best interest to ignore such trivialities. I tried to reason with my parents, citing obvious incompatibility with the suitors of their choice and the threat a rushed marriage would pose to my burgeoning career, but all to no avail. They were relentless in their conviction.

The tussle was still on when a foreign element was introduced in our midst – the ash smeared figure with breaded hair, clad in black overalls. He materialized at our door chanting verses in an unfamiliar language with a hoarseness befitting his frightening persona. I cringed at the mere sight of him. His advent had been manifested as a chance happening, but it beggared my belief to attribute it to mere coincidence.

The man looked at my hand, stared at my forehead, made some damning prophesies about calamities that would befall our family if I did not get married within the next six months and left clutching an envelope that I figured was brimming with currency notes. What a waste, I mused, as my parents resumed their assault with a renewed vigor. It was as though the despicable man had been a supplier of performance enhancing drugs. He definitely looked the part.

The house had turned into a battleground of sorts with each side scheming and plotting to prove their ideological supremacy over the other, only I was left alone to fend for myself. On one hand my mother would attempt to lure me through compassion and tenderness and on the other my father would rely on his stringency for my surrender. I was tired of ducking unexpected volleys from people I had never found a reason to be weary of and this had been eroding something deep within my being. It was for the first time in my life that I was feeling so lonely in my own house and in the company of my own parents. I had contemplated telling them about Vishal, but they seemed too preoccupied with their motive to give me even a willing ear. I was no longer sure about them or how they would react to this piece of news and so for the sake of harmony I refrained from bringing up the subject.

The telling blow for my composure came when my father coaxed me into meeting one of his business associate's sons. I had warned him about the futility of the exercise in advance, but he had been adamant and despite my reluctance, invited the family over for lunch. Like a mannequin on display, I was decked up in a glittering Saree and made to serve tea and Pakoras to the guests – a task I went about in the utmost mechanical fashion - before I was permitted to join them.

As the discussion rallied around various topics of diverse nature, I could feel probing eyes of the entire family – the boy and his oversized parents - boring through me. Discomforting as it was, I endured the ordeal without flinching or participating in the conversation. The family ran a successful printing press in Rajkot and the boy, I forget his name, was the only heir to their booming enterprise. He looked like a human version of a Chihuahua, not in terms of the cuteness quotient but purely the looks. He was petite and boney and when he smiled or tried to speak, his jaws protruded in a bizarre manner.

Later, at the lunch table, I even noticed a healthy residue of chewing tobacco lining up the base of his teeth. The sight was disgusting and I was left wondering if my parents had actually met the fellow earlier and short listed him as a prospective groom for me or had he been a surprise even for them. I looked at my father and then my mother, but they were totally engrossed in feeding the guests, forcing a Puri or a serving of Undhiyu on their already bursting plates. I felt a rush of fury run through me. Why were my parents behaving so gutlessly? If the guests wanted another helping they could help themselves and if they didn't, well, so be it. They were highly unlikely to starve in the foreseeable future, the parents at least if not the son. What was then all the farce about? And what was I doing there anyways?

After the main course we shifted back to the sitting area where the desserts were served, an array of home made delicacies and sweets. We Gujaratis' love our sweets. As I fought my self-imposed restraint, permitting myself to savor 'only' some from the spread of treats, one after the other the elders exited from the scene. 'You kids should talk a bit. It is important for you to get to know each other,' were my mothers last comments before she followed suit with her own disappearing act.

A discomfiting silence ensued and when it was finally broken I prayed for it to come back. 'Sejal Ben, so what do you do in

Mumbai?' he said in the typical Kathiawadi dialect. Immediately my abhorrence for him shot up a notch. Though the 'Ben' suffix was commonplace when it came to addressing women in Gujarat, it was the first time that I had heard someone address me with it. It sounded atrocious. The man never stood a chance with me in the first place and now, by simply opening his mouth, he had doused any scope even for a civil dialogue. I sat there muted, nodding my head when absolutely necessary and waiting for the nightmare to end.

'So, what do you think of him?' within a few minutes of the guests departing, my father confronted me. Tragically for him, this was exactly the kind of fissure that the fury welled up within me had been wanting.

'Have you lost your mind? Or, have you simply turned blind? How can you even think of marrying me with a moron like that? Or, have I become too much of a burden on you?' I screamed. 'Why? What's wrong with him?' he shot back, bettering my pitch.

'Stop it you two. And Seju, this is not how you are supposed to speak to your father. We are only doing what we think is in your best interest. How can you even think that you have become a burden for us?' my mother interjected, quickly slipping into a pool of tears. Her tears were a weapon I had seldom seen wasted for as long back as I could remember; a tact that I was yet to pick up from her. But my wounds were much deeper; it was not going to be simple for her tears to wash them away this time round.

'What is the welfare you have in mind by wanting to marry me off to that tobacco-chewing maggot?' I replied, this time with some degree of composure. 'He is a nice boy from a well to do family. We know them for years and I am sure he will keep you happy. But if you don't like him, that's a different matter altogether. Tell us the kind of boy you want and we will try to find one that meets your expectations. Or if there is anyone particular you have in mind, let us know and we can initiate dialogue with the family.'

My screaming it seemed had finally got them within the realms of reason. This was the first opening I had got since I came home and though the situation was not the most conducive, I didn't want to let go of it. 'Ma, I told you that I am not ready to marry just as yet, but if I do need to get married, it can't be with someone who is so... so... different from me. It has to be someone who will understand me and support me in achieving my career goals, someone who thinks the way I do and lives life the way I like to lead mine.'

'So, is there someone like that who you have in your life already?' she interjected. Something in my speech must have betrayed my intent as she was now looking at me with a strange glint in her eyes. My father too had ceased emitting fumes and was listening to the conversation intently. 'His name is Vishal...' I began, transferring all information about him I thought to be material, within a span of a few minutes.

'And what is he?' my father finally spoke. No, it wasn't Vishal's evolutionary antecedents that he was interested in. He had this habit of dropping vague sounding questions and statements every now and then, but I was his daughter and if anyone was genetically programmed to get his drift, it was me. 'He is a Punjabi,' I replied.

'Punjabi!' he exclaimed and within moments the balance which had started to descend on his frontage had evaporated. 'Hundreds and thousands of eligible Gujarati boys around and you end up picking up a Punjabi for yourself. Have you absolutely no concern left for your family? Or absorbed in your selfishness you forgot to think about us completely? How do you think we will face the society? Or do you want us to move about concealing our faces for the rest of our lives?'

One thing led to the other and we were soon spilling our guts out on each other. I knew that the society we hailed from was a conservative one, but my father's stance reminded me of the words from Henry Ford's autobiography, 'Any customer can have a car painted any color that he wants so long as it is black.'

Agreed that being my father he had every right to interfere in crucial matters governing my life, but I deserved a say at least, if not more. I could not afford to let myself be bulldozed by his authoritarianism and bear the brunt of my cowardice for my remaining years. Moreover, I was now in serious doubts about his intentions as well. Was he genuinely concerned about my wellbeing or was he simply playing to his ego? What was more important to him, his daughter's happiness or ridding himself of his social obligation to get me married? Given that he was eager to marry me off to the creep he had invited for lunch, could I still afford to live under the impression that he understood me well enough to be the sole custodian of my interests?

I reached Mumbai with a day to spare before I was required to join work and I chose to spend it catching up on some much needed rest. The overnight bus journey had been tiring and I retreated to the bed within minutes of entering the house. Kamini wasn't in and I resisted the temptation to call and check on her. I wasn't in the mood to explain my premature arrival and all the invigorations that had led to it. My brain was numb with exhaustion and I didn't want to burden it any further.

Solitude, they say, is an amplifier for one's emotions and it wasn't long before it started streaming rancorous thoughts to fill the void in my head. I thought about my father's rigid and thoughtless stance, feeling disappointed; I thought about the obnoxious character that had come seeking my hand in marriage, feeling disgusted; and I tried to visualize the life that would have beckoned had I buckled under pressure, feeling terrified. I was not able to sleep, not able to close my eyes even, and subsequently I gave up, opting to get out of the house instead.

I needed some kind of an engagement, just about anything that would keep my mind off my prickling thoughts. Aimlessly I hailed an auto and directed the driver to drop me off at Linking Road in Bandra. This was a prominent shopping district of the city and though I had involuntarily opted for the destination, I already had a reasonably long mental list of things to be checked out by the time I got down from the auto. I paid the fare and turned towards the sidewalk when suddenly a bright signage caught my attention.

'Tattoo Studio – get yourself inked by experienced artists from Miami,' the words on the signage read. Right next to the text was an image of a model exhibiting a large multi-colored reptile that seemed to be wrapped around her entire bare back. The image was noticeable, even attention grabbing, but not particularly attractive. 'I would never go for something so huge; it is too much of overkill. Something more subtle, a small butterfly or flower may be,' I thought, carefully studying the design on the model's back.

Tattoos had always fascinated me. As a child I had often seen women from the nearby villages adorning crude, paling inscriptions on various parts of their body, often names of their husbands or religious symbols, and found them immensely intriguing. Especially the Rabbari women with magical symbols tattooed on the neck, breasts and arms had never ceased to fascinate me. But I had never ever considered getting one for myself. Even as a child I had known that tattoos were not for 'us'. Women from 'our' families were not supposed to get themselves inked. I had never asked as to who the 'us' were and I wasn't sure if I knew the answer even now.

Unlike the big-city perception of them being a domain for thugs, delinquents or rebels, in my hometown tattoos were yet another tool for feudalistic differentiation. They lacked the rebellious appeal that attracts hundreds of big-city youths to tattoo parlors and hence had always remained a thing to be admired from a distance for me. But if there was a time that I wanted to let go of the values that folks from smaller towns mercilessly clung on to, like my own parents, it was now. I was ready to plunge out of their word; a world of antiquated and obsolete ethos and with a smile I entered the forbidden tract behind the doors of the studio.

After a teeth-gritting, excruciating hour, I emerged, feeling satiated with a gay abandon that had eluded me for a while now. I small butterfly in red, green and black was affixed on my chest at just the spot where, by a simple choice of garment, I could choose to exhibit or conceal it at will. The experience of getting a tattoo had been painful and far more expensive than what I had anticipated, but it was totally worth it. Despite the clearly visible abrasions on my skin I liked what I saw and I was eager to flaunt my prized possession to Kamini and Vishal. I had taken another step away from the city I had left the previous evening and I was feeling much lighter in the head now.

On Wednesday morning while I was waiting for the lift to descend, I saw Gaurav walk in through the lobby. By the time he saw me he had already taken a few strides towards the lift. Suddenly he paused, his eyes simmering like a barbeque grill, almost ready to assault me with the burning coal, and abruptly turned towards the staircase. The marketing team was relegated to the fifth floor of the building, quite a climb from the ground floor lobby. I smiled to myself. Clearly, the reason for his sudden appetite for exercise was me and I wasn't complaining.

I had an e-mail from Kavita waiting in my inbox, asking me to see her once I was back in office. If Gaurav's conduct was an indication, something had surely transpired while I was away and curious for more, I immediately headed towards her cabin.

'I spoke with Gaurav and obviously he had a somewhat different version of the story to tell,' she started without wasting a single word. I opened my mouth to interject but was made to shut up by a slight sway of her hand. 'This is bound to happen. A conflict exists only when there are two different perspectives or opinions, and for a suitable resolution it is important that both are paid a heed to,' she explained. I could feel my nerves tensing and my stomach clenching. Was it possible that Gaurav had convinced her about my story not being the accurate account of events? Had I left some glaring loophole that had made Kavita believe him over me? But soon my concerns were settled.

'But all that is not important and this is exactly what I told him as well. The fact is that both of you concede that something unwarranted did happen and the only options I am left with are either to raise the issue with Compliance and get them to conduct a comprehensive investigation into your allegations or to amicably resolve the issue. Knowing how these investigations proceed, it won't be easy tidings for either of you and Gaurav agrees with me. So, he is fine with shifting to a different circle with immediate effect, if that suits you?'

I took my time to reply. His transfer would mean that I wouldn't have to endure his antics any more, but that wasn't enough. I couldn't permit the bastard to be let off the hook so conveniently. 'That is fine Kavita, but... I mean, he does all of this and gets away with merely a job transfer? You think this is fair?' I spoke mildly, measuring the words as they emerged from my lips.

'No, he is not being let off easily. Gaurav was due for a promotion and since he will now be shifting laterally, he will have to work his way all over again in the new circle to even be considered for a promotion. It sets his career back by at least a year and half or two. His sufferings might be mild in comparison with yours but they are substantial nevertheless. It won't ease your pain and I can't commit a fixed timeframe, but I will also try and get something nice for you from your career's perspective. This is the best I can do from my side,' she said, looking at me expectantly.

Her inclination to settle the issue amicably was understandable since an investigation would not only leave a blotch on the team she was directly responsible for, but would also draw up heavily in terms of time and resources. I had started to live the image of the hapless prey that I had inadvertently painted in my own selfish interest, but the fact was that Gaurav wasn't as guilty as I was making him out to be and the verdict was as favorable as I had originally wanted it to be. So, after displaying some minor inhibitions I took up the offer, but not before I made it amply clear that I was acceding only because Kavita wanted me to. She was the division head and I was no longer naïve enough to let go of an opportunity to appease her. Moreover, hadn't she promised that she would try and do something for me? Who knows how much of a difference these little things would make to what that 'something' eventually turned out to be.

The great suffocating cloud that had been crushing me had lifted and I felt an urgent need to blow off the steam. Before leaving office I called up Vishal to check if he happened to be in the same part of town. He wasn't, so we agreed to meet up at my place a little later. I had met Vishal last evening as well and as expected, he had almost flipped at the sight of my tattoo. 'Amazing,' was all he uttered, continuing to stare at the body-art till I had to literally snap him out of his trance. It was slightly awkward to have him stare brazenly at my breast in full view of the other patrons at the coffee shop where we were sitting.

Soon the discussion swiveled towards my visit to Rajkot and I felt all my excitement being drained away. As I summarized my failure to convince my parents, I felt my grief and gloom returning with a renewed vigor. The evening had lost its magic and by the time I was through with the story, I was itching to return home. I had once again switched to the leave-me-alone mode and as a result, our date was forced to come to an abrupt end. Today I was feeling happy and wanted to make it up to him. I had something special in mind – another shock - and once again I was eager to see his reaction.

'When do you want to get married?' I shot out even before he had completed lodging himself on the chair. 'What?' he exclaimed, looking at me as though he had just seen a ghost. 'You heard me, when do you want to get married?' I replied.

'What do you mean?' he muttered, looking thoroughly puzzled. I was enjoying the role of a tease and he looked kind of cute, trying to make some sense out of my words. 'Arey, barely a few days back you were all buckle-kneed, trying to force a ring up my finger and now when I ask you about marriage you feign ignorance. Do you want to get married to me in the first place or not?'

He heaved a sigh of relief as his wavelength matched up to my words. 'Oh… of course, I want to marry you,' he replied. 'So let's do it then, what are we waiting for?' I added. I had just taken my second step away from my parents and their bourgeois beliefs and I wasn't feeling one bit remorseful. In fact I was once against feeling the lightness of freedom, like a bird in its unrestrained flight, and it was indeed a wonderful feeling.

FIFTEEN

Vishal did not waste much time in breaking the news to his folks and it was then I realized that conservatism was perhaps a thing embedded within the mould used to create the preceding generation of humans and my parents were not the only ones carrying its burden around. Agreed, Vishal had severed some threads from his ties with his parents with a bid to pursue a career in acting, but given their big-city antecedents, neither of us had expected the response we got from them.

It is no secret that the word Gujarati is as demeaning to a thoroughbred Punjabi as Punjabi is for Gujaratis. Harmonious coexistence in public is another matter, but when it comes to taking the association any further, both sections are known to repel in a manner that could put like magnetic poles to shame. We were however banking on the supposed open mindedness of his parents and the excitement that the news of their son's impending marriage was likely to bring, to help us get their buy in.

As per Vishal, his mother had sounded excited when he had mentioned his willingness to take the conjugal plunge and she had immediately begun to suggest names of girls for his consideration. Only when he had interjected a few times and repeated that there was already a girl he had in mind that she relented, but only to ambush him with a fresh volley of questions about me. She seemed glad to hear that I wasn't engaged in the same line of work as her son and apparently she even sounded impressed with my academic qualifications.

It was when the word Gujarati was introduced into the conversation that all hell broke loose. His mother went hysterical, ranting about how their social standing had already been compromised with Vishal's decision to become an actor and that his decision to marry a 'Gujju Girl' would be the last nail in the coffin of their social existence. 'How can you be so heartless? How can you not think about us at all? What will we tell people?' she had pleaded with him, but Vishal had exhibited remarkable tact in dealing with the situation.

He had calmly informed her that his decision was nonnegotiable and the only options that remained for them were to either be a part of the wedding or not. I felt he was being a tad harsh but he knew his folks better and his display of apathy yielded surprising results. A few days later he received a call from his father, clearly the more levelheaded among his parents, who explained their predicament to him and said that given the societal constraints they would not be in a position to host the marriage in Delhi but they will surely come down to Mumbai to participate in it. He also offered Vishal some money for the expenses, which he summarily declined to accept.

The implication was clear. It had to be just the two of us who were left to plan and execute our own marriage. Instead of going about the traditional route of engaging a priest to come up with an auspicious date, we settled for 14th February instead. What better day than Saint Valentine's to tie the nuptial knot? Except that we were left with barely a month to make all the arrangements.

We settled for a small ceremony in a local temple, primarily for the satisfaction of Vishal's parents, followed by a party for our friends. Having seen my parent's reaction once, I had refrained from engaging them during the planning phase, lest they renewed their attempts to make me change my mind. Instead I had opted to send them one of the few wedding cards we had printed, which I did with only about a week to go for the marriage. I knew that this would douse any thoughts of attending the wedding that they might come up with and that is exactly the way I wanted it to be. The last thing I wanted was to call upon another distraction that would prevent me from relishing this special moment of my life.

The days preceding our marriage went by in the customary preoccupations of making the basic arrangements, hunting for a house where we could shift together, making it livable within our budgetary constraints and shopping. Amid the ruckus I managed to squeeze some time to get an affidavit made for a change of name and get a notification published in two local dailies as per the provisions of the law. I wanted to get away from my past and my orthodox name was one constant reminder of it that I had vowed to get rid of. The timing was opportune and the new heterodox name, Sherlyn, that I had opted for had a nice ring to it, more attuned to the spirit of the life I thought I was embarking upon.

Vishal too had concurred with my choice of name and as a result, on the day after the marriage ceremony in the temple, we walked out of the Bandra Family Court with a certificate pronouncing Vishal and Sherlyn Ahuja man and wife. Kamini and another one of our common friends had been our two witnesses.

Within days of my joining work post marriage, I found an envelope waiting for me at my desk. 'Congratulations! In light of the exemplary performance in your current role, you are herewith promoted to the level of Assistant Manager – Marketing,' was its opening line. Kavita had lived up to her word and it was a great start to my married life. Post the marriage expenses, both Vishal's and my bank balances were dwindling and we could do with the sizeable increment that accompanied my promotion. I was ecstatic and could not wait to share the news with 'my husband'. It was odd to refer to Vishal as my husband but I was enjoying the part of getting used to it.

We had rented a one bedroom flat very close to the one that I had been sharing with Kamini. It worked well for both of us since it was close to the studios and production houses that Vishal had to frequent and it was also the one area in the city that I was intimately familiar with. Kamini had been highly supportive of my decision to marry Vishal and in fact she was the one who had broached the topic of my moving out. 'Where are you guys thinking of shifting?' she had casually quizzed.

It was a matter that had been troubling me for a while and yet I hadn't been able to muster enough courage to bring it up with her. 'Meaning?' I responded, feigning ignorance.

'What 'meaning'? You guys are not planning to shift in with me, are you? In case you are nurturing any freak fantasies, let me set the records straight – I am not much into orgies,' she had teased. She had helped us finalize the house and later, in setting it up, with an enthusiasm that did well to conceal any disappointment she was feeling over losing a roommate. 'Wasn't I managing on my own before you came? Don't worry, I will be fine,' she had said when I expressed my guilt on having to abandon her. The proximity of our new abode to Kamini's also helped in checking my wave of guilt.

It wasn't a particularly large place but we had made it out into a nice cozy pad with extremely modern furnishing. The marriage and the house interiors had left us with little money to plan a real honeymoon, so we had spent the few days following our marriage holed up in the house and quenching our thirst for each other's company. It was like our very own paradise of shared solitude. We would take turns cooking for each other and very often end up making out on the kitchen slab, leaving the unprepared meal to be tended to later.

The juncture of marriage had recalibrated the bond Vishal and I had shared and suddenly we found ourselves engaging in mushy squabbles and romantic sessions of simply staring at each other. Even our lovemaking had not been left untouched. Vishal had lost some of his aggression and went about exploring me with a newfound caring gentleness, strangely though, but a development even I found myself appreciating. Joining work after this blissful reprieve was piquing, but the unexpected promotion had made my day. I was suddenly eager to wind up and return home to Vishal and to the pad that we had lovingly decorated.

I did manage to get out of office just in time to beat the peak hour traffic and reached home only to be greeted by the padlock dangling on the door hinge. I was disappointed and also slightly surprised. Vishal had not mentioned that he would be going out and neither had he called or sent a text message to inform me of his plans. The disappointment didn't last long and realizing the irrationality of my reaction, I was quick to brush it aside. I prepared a cup of tea and parked myself on a beanbag in front of the television. 'He doesn't have to inform me every time he steps out of the house. How juvenile of me to even think of such a thing,' I told myself.

But as dinner time approached and there was still no news of Vishal, I started getting anxious and tried to reach him on his mobile. 'The number you are trying to reach is out of coverage area,' a pre-recorded and awfully irritating voice informed me each time I dialed his number. I left a couple of messages and waited for him for as long as my grumbling tummy would permit and then I went ahead and had my dinner, alone, for the first time since our marriage. I was just about ready to retire to the bedroom when the doorbell rang. I looked at the wall clock, it said 11.15 p.m.

I had intended to retain my frown till such time that he apologized for subjecting me to the anxious wait, but as soon as I opened the door, I was forced to wipe it off my face. Standing close on his heels was Kamini and both of them were carrying shopping bags of various shapes and hues. 'Hi baby. How was your day?' he said, reaching out to embrace me, bags dangling from both his hands. 'Hi,' I replied as he receded, leaving behind a faint whiff of alcohol.

'How are you darling?' Kamini was quick to push him aside and take her turn at pouncing on me. 'I know you are newly married and all that, but that doesn't mean that you need to completely disappear,' she added. She was sounding genuinely excited to see me and I was glad to see her too. I hadn't realized, but it had been more than a week that we had not seen each other. I moved aside, allowing them to enter the house. My mood had sobered down considerably but I couldn't help but ask them as to where they had been.

'I was getting bored at home so I called her and since she too had a day off we decided to go out shopping. Now don't be a spoilsport; stop sulking and see what all we have got. Here, isn't this the kind of cushion you wanted for the settee? And look at this,' he said, fishing out a t-shirt from one of the packets. 'Is this for me?' I asked. 'Obviously! You don't expect me to wear a fuchsia pink tee, do you?'

The garment was indeed pretty and I was still checking it out, searching for the right words of praise when Kamini playfully punched him on his shoulder. 'Hello! Don't gobble up all the credit. Whose choice was it?' she said.

The playful banter continued as one after the other they emptied all the bags, revealing their contents and fighting over which one of them had picked up a particular item and who had done well to drive a great bargain. Kamini had bought a couple of Kurtas and tops while Vishal had bought some household items that we had discussed the need for, a book that I had been wanting to pick up for a while, a t-shirt and denims for himself and the pink t-shirt and a blue Kurta for me. The kurta was nice too and once again the war to claim the credit for picking it up had remained inconclusive.

Left to me I would have stalled the splurging for a few months and waited for a few cheques to get liquidated into our bank accounts, but the nobility of Vishal's intentions were beyond doubt. My heart was once again brimming with love for my husband and the discomfort I had felt due to his unexpected absence had become a thing of the past. At the opportune moment I broke the news of my promotion, leaving Vishal ecstatic and Kamini happy. 'This, we need to celebrate,' he said, dishing out a box of choco-chip cookies – my favorite - from one of the yet unopened shopping bags. Animatedly he rushed to the kitchen and emerged with three glasses, an ice bucket and a bottle of Vodka.

The drinking session extended well into the night and at about 2.00 Kamini expressed her desire to head back home. It was late and she was drunk, obviously not the best combination for a lonely girl to walk the city streets. So, upon our insistence, she too crashed over at our place for the night.

That night I went to bed feeling good about life in general and my husband in particular. He was so alive, so fun loving and so considerate, just the kind of partner that young girls from rural India spend days fasting for. The last thing I wanted was to cramp him for space and drown his vitality in my misplaced expectations and this was the first resolve I made towards the protraction of my marital bliss. The next morning, despite the ceaseless hammering I could feel in my head, I recalled my resolve and once again vowed to abide by it. Vishal and Kamini were both sound asleep by the time I left to endure another day at the office.

My marriage too, like what I had heard of marriages to be, was divided into two distinct phases. The first phase of blessedness and beatitude where one discovers various facets to ones partner and finds them endearing, lasted for a little over a year. Vishal remained his familiar jovial self, forcing me to smile even at the bleakest of moments. We would party hard, weekends and weekdays alike, drinking and making merry with one set of friends or the other.

Marriage seemed to have brought about a renewed sense of responsibility in him and he had intensified his efforts at finding work in the chaos called the film and television industry. His efforts were not going unrewarded and the number of ad films and television appearances coming his way were on a steady rise. Though his dream of acting on the big screen still remained elusive, his career graph did not leave us with much to complain about.

For me it was a distinct high to watch him on television and tell my colleagues at work about the next endorsement he had bagged. Since most of my colleagues were connected with the entertainment industry only as enthusiastic audiences, the reflective admiration they showered upon me due to my husband's vocation was something I had started to get accustomed to. 'Wow, he looks so hot with his grunge look in the new deodorant ad. But, don't you get jealous watching him get intimate with such hot looking babes?' one of the girls would innocently ask every once in a while and I would go on to explain how he was a professional and this, his livelihood. 'Why would it matter to me? Eventually it is me that he has to come home to,' I would exultingly reply.

I had always known Vishal to be a caring and level headed person, but once I found myself at the center of all his attention, I couldn't help but thank my stars for landing him in my lap. His odd work hours meant that there were times when he would return home much after I had gone to bed or not return at all, but he continued to pamper me with small things that meant the world to me. On days I would get up with a rose next to my pillow or a small gift on the bed side table and I couldn't help but look at his sleeping face and smile. A leaking faucet or a bulb that needed to be replaced or any such thing that I would have been planning to tend to would suddenly be working fine when I returned from work and once again I would be forced to smile to myself.

At times when due to excessive pressure at work I ended up ignoring my meals or my health in general, he would scold me, bringing back memories from my childhood when my parents would do the same. My parents had not attempted to contact me since I had sent my wedding card to them and though I had no complaints with the life I had chosen, there were times that I remembered and missed them. And at such times, when I was feeling low, feeling the void of my estranged parents, he would be the one to bring me back to life by a funny remark or simply a warm embrace.

It wasn't a sudden transition, but once the euphoria of marriage settled, I felt our relationship establishing itself into a zone of maturity and understanding. The cozy, mushy, emotionally heightened moments had declined in their occurrences and instead most matters started to get weighed on a scale of practicality.

His unexpected acts that had surprised me earlier had slipped within the periphery of my expectations and would often go unnoticed. Instead, it was when he would miss doing something that he would have done earlier that it would come to my notice. If there was a party he had to attend during the week, I would opt to stay back instead of accompanying him and struggling with a hangover at work the next morning. His indulgences and spend-thriftiness ceased to appeal to me as well-intended cute acts and though never enough to confront him, I found myself grappling with a mild degree of irritation due to them. His ways had begun to seem somewhat bohemian to me rather than the spirited approach towards life they had been earlier.

It wasn't anything flagrant or worrisome, it was just a relationship seeking out its comfort zone and both of us had involuntarily attuned ourselves to its altering form. We still had our longings for each other, we still went out during weekends and had fun in each others company, only instead of young and impulsive individuals we were now a maturing couple.

In one of the tabloids, I had stumbled upon a scientific explanation for our transitioning relationship. It said that the initial, obsessive state of love is accompanied by a host of chemical changes in our body – the release of Dopamine that gives one the same high as being on cocaine or nicotine, and the gush of adrenaline, resulting in increased heartbeats and restless excitement. Once the chemically-laden internal tempest settles, a confident, stable love takes over from an uncertain, excited and nervous romance.

It was in this settled phase of my marriage that I sought out to seek a job change. Not that I was facing any difficulties at my current workplace, but my job was beginning to get monotonous. After my last promotion I had reached the highest level that one could expect to scale in my current profile, ruling out a vertical movement unless I settled for a role change. And since I had not completed even two years from my last promotion I could not bring myself to approach Kavita for a role change or another promotion so soon.

The search didn't take long and within a couple of months I had an offer letter from one of other players in the telecom space to join them as a Marketing Manager for their Maharashtra & Goa circle. They were giving me a sizeable jump over my current remuneration; a fact which when coupled with the craving for novelty in my monotonous professional life helped me arrive at my decision without much deliberations.

SIXTEEN

My induction into the new workplace was accompanied by the customary components - anxiety, nervousness and groping eyes of my new male colleagues. Sometimes I wonder if it would be wise for the women walking into a new workplace to be issued a temporary identity card reading 'Opportunity', till such time that all interested males have all exhausted their attempts to impress her. As any decent looking girl would agree, this over-friendliness and extra attention can be extremely unnerving at times.

To my dismay, Srinivas Murthy, my new boss, also happened to be on the list of my recently acquired admirers. 'Sherlyn! What a lovely name. You know, the minute I read it on your resume, I knew that this was the girl I wanted on my team,' were his opening words when I entered his cabin, reporting for my first day at the new office. He was dark complexioned, the kinds you would not want to engage in a game of hide-and-seek, with a receding hairline and blunt features.

To his credit, he could boast of a fit body, but that was the least and also the best he could do to make himself somewhat presentable.

Initially I found his flirtatious remarks mildly annoying but as time went by I found myself adjusting to them and taking them in my stride. Srini, as he was generally referred to, was one of the most regarded individuals in office. Even the circle head, his boss, measured his words while addressing him. Srini had years of experience under his belt and it had been his marketing acumen that was largely responsible for turning around the fortunes of the company in the region. The company had been a modest number four player, content and comfortable, only a couple of years back and then Srini had taken over the reigns of Marketing for the circle.

He designed various ambush marketing campaigns, luring customers to give up their loyalties and switch networks and even before the competitors could rise from their slumber, the company's subscriber base was pressing on the heels of the market leader. And if his competencies and intellect left any doubts about his stronghold, they were surely settled by the fact that he was a distant cousin of the Country CEO of the company. Srini was a big man and I can't claim with much certainty, but this might have acted as a catalyst in the brisk adjustment I had made with his ways – laughing on his loaded remarks and saying just enough to keep the candle of hope blazing for him while maintaining enough distance to prevent my own fingers from burning.

You might find it strange, but I think I had even started to enjoy our frivolous banter. And no, before you start accusing me of adultery or any other such heinous crime, let me set the record straight that nothing of that sort was transpiring. Vishal knew all about my relationship with Srini. In fact whenever there was any notable exchange of such teasing words between Srini and me, I made it a point to share it with Vishal, testing him for any reactions that could act as a guide for me. I didn't quite know as to why I felt the need to share Srini's banter with Vishal, our marital accord was way beyond being susceptible to such trivialities and I had no misgivings about it.

Vishal had retained his former exterior of being flirty and coquettish, almost to the point of being a tease for the more vulnerable girls, through the nearly three years of our marriage. Irrespective of my presence, he uninhibitedly flirted with his colleagues and friends and somehow it didn't seem to matter to me. I had seen enough married men swearing on their dedication and loyalty, only to make a fully conscious slip at the first available opportunity. I had been with enough men to know the difference between attraction, physical desire and the special bond that we shared – true love.

Vishal loved me and that was the only thing that mattered. I had accepted him the way he was and I knew that it would be unfair on my part to use the leverage of marriage to seek any adjustments to his personality. I had the option of ignoring and looking the other way, but I preferred instead to look life straight in the eye. It didn't matter to me if he flirted with a hundred women or, strange as it may sound, slept with half of them. We were married for three years now and our relationship had matured to a level where there was no room for insecurity induced possessiveness.

Vishal too made no attempts to hide anything from me. If he was hanging out with a girl and I happened to ask him about his whereabouts or the matter simply came up during a conversation, he would tell me exactly where and who he was with. Only, I refrained from being too inquisitive and he avoided volunteering too many details, especially the more intimate ones. We were leading a happy married life with abundant space to allow each other to approach life in the fashion each one desired and yet I felt an overbearing compulsion to talk to Vishal about Srini. Perhaps it was some hidden guilt within me which sought his explicit approval for my meandering rather than the tacit one that formed the core of our companionship.

As expected, Vishal never complained. If anything, he laughed with me at the lame lines Srini came up with and this encouraged me to tease Srini further. 'You know, today during lunch we were talking about drinking and he was boasting about his capacity for alcohol consumption. I told him that maybe he hadn't met the right competition yet and that I could take him on any day. He didn't believe me and was willing to put a wager on it,' I shared with Vishal one evening. 'Well, he doesn't know who he is messing with,' he was quick to respond. 'Actually, you know what; you should take him up on the challenge. Just get him to up the stakes to something worthwhile – maybe a promotion or a sizeable increment or something - and then show him what drinking actually means. What say?'

Encouraged by Vishal's pepping, I did take on Srini for the bet. However, I could not bring myself to mention the stakes my husband had suggested and instead we left the prize to be decided by the one who emerged victorious. The venue, in accordance with my adversary's stature, was a lounge bar at one of the suburban five star hotels. Or maybe he had opted for the place hoping to use their residential facilities later, who knows. We started with a couple of tequila shots before moving to our standard drinks, vodka for me and single malt for him. We could keep count for a while, post which we resorted to ordering both refills together to keep a tab on who consumed how many drinks. We were both drinking rapidly, focusing on the contest at hand rather than any peripheral banter and in no time I could feel a distinct slur in the words I spoke. To my delight, he wasn't faring any better.

'You know... you know... your lips, they are so luscious... just like... mmm... strawberries,' he said in a manner that made me laugh. 'I feel like kissing you. Can I?' he added.

The drinks, all our past flirtations, his clout within the organization, my husband's consent for our date – the concoction was heady enough to make me concede much more than just a kiss, but I decided against letting myself flow with the wave for once. 'But I am married and so are you... Is this some sort of an indecent proposal then?' I made a feeble attempt at humor.

'Indecent? Why indecent? We are both adults and I felt like kissing you so I said so. Now if you feel the same, you can say a yes, else never mind. Simple, isn't it? Why do you have to complicate it by bringing our marriage... and what not, in between?' his argument made some sense. And even if it didn't, what the heck! We were soon cuddled up on the sofa, kissing like lovebirds deprived of an opportune place to make out. He did suggest that we take our endeavor upstairs to one of the rooms, 'I know people here and getting a room wont be a hassle,' he claimed, but something within me did well to curb my alcohol infested desires. It wasn't the right time, I told myself. I had learnt my lessons well and even in my inebriated state a part of me was aware that when it came to men, the worst thing a girl could do was to make it 'easy'.

It was the chase and not the conquest that men pleasured from and if I was to remain in any position of command, I had to pace Srini's chase right. 'No, this is enough for now. Let's save some things for later,' I said. I can only imagine how Srini must have felt. He pleaded, begged, reasoned and did everything in his might to convince me. He was so desperate that at that moment I could have made him do anything, make him bark like a dog, promise me a promotion or just about anything else. I remained relentless, basking in my newfound power over him, and ignoring his most frantic pleas I called for the Check.

By the time his car turned into the gates of my apartment complex, Srini was already snoring away to glory. Thankfully his driver knew his job well and so I was reasonably confident of him reaching home in one piece.

I was slightly perplexed to see the lights of our flat switched on. It was three a.m. and if Vishal was home, he should have been asleep by now. I rummaged through my bag for my set of keys and opened the door, only to find him watching some wildlife program on Discovery channel. 'Welcome back. So how was the date?' he asked with a teasing smile. 'Shut up!' I replied, blushing. 'What date and all? It was nice... but just an outing. No date-shate.'

'Ok Baba, only outing... happy? How was it but?'

'I told him all about the evening – the drinks we had, the topics we discussed and eventually, the kiss as well. 'That's it? Nothing happened beyond that?' I was perplexed at his question. I didn't know what exactly, but I was expecting some degree of dissent from him, a reaction of sorts, and instead he was sounding disturbingly normal. He was asking me if anything else had happened as though I were narrating an episode from some daily soap. I was surprised and somewhat disappointed, but maybe he was doing a much better job of giving me space in our marriage than I was.

Our little encounter didn't change anything between Srini and me. For the first couple of days he attempted to rope me in for another 'outing', but when I successfully wiggled out each time, he grudgingly gave up his attempts. He remained the flirtatious boss that everyone knew him to be and I reciprocated, just as I had been doing in the past.

Today, almost a month after our first encounter, except for the one team dinner he had invited us to his place for, he had made a clumsy attempt to invite me home. He had messaged me on the office chat network asking me about my plans for the evening, with just a passing mention of his wife being away. The overture wasn't explicit since he did mention that his kids would be glad to have me visit, but the hint was too obvious to be missed. Initially I was tempted to take up the offer since our previous meeting had left a few unfulfilled desires at my end too, but at the last minute I checked myself to turn it down. It was still a tad early, I thought.

It was clear that the desire to have me was still burning strong inside him and it was in this state of heightened anxiety that Srini could prove to be most beneficial for me. The next appraisal cycle was due and there was an outside chance that a well played card could elevate me to the position of a Senior Manager. A possibility I couldn't afford to ruin because of some childish infatuation that was bubbling within me. I returned home, still thinking whether turning down his invite was the right thing to do or did I just close my doors to an opportunity of getting him to commit to my promotion within the seclusion of his bedroom. And not to mention the itch to feel him close to me, on top of me, that I had been struggling with for some time now.

'You wouldn't believe where we are going tomorrow,' Vishal exclaimed excitedly as soon as I entered the house. Odd that he was home on a Friday evening, I was half expecting him to be out partying, as was the case on most Fridays, and return only once I had resigned to deep sleep. 'Where are we going?' I asked, unable to bring the right ring of enthusiasm in my voice. Perhaps the long and exhausting day at work had drained a part of my ability to express myself.

'Imtiyaz Khan, the director, we are going to his party,' he said, sounding ecstatic. 'This is like a dream. I had met him some time back through a friend of mine… Sekhar, you know him, don't you? The music director fellow who we had bumped into at the X-Lounge?'

I only had a vague recollection about Sekhar, but I nodded in agreement. 'Yesterday I met Sekhar again; he is working in Imtiyaz's next movie. He told me about this party that Imtiyaz was hosting for a select group of friends and promised to get me an invite if he could. Today he called saying that we are on the guest list. Yippie,' he screamed. I couldn't recall the last time when I had seen him so jubilant. But I did understand his joy and the possible implications of this seemingly inconsequential party invite towards fulfilling his ambitions.

Over the past three years of our marriage I had seen Vishal tide over uncertainties and challenges inherent to his chosen field of work, always with a smile. I was confident of his abilities, but given the disorderly nature in which the entertainment industry functioned, there were times when I permitted slivers of doubt to seep into my thoughts. Contrastingly I had not once seen him harboring any reservations about his success. It was as though he knew that his success was preordained and he was only biding time, waiting for the stars to align favorably. His persistence and hope rode on his dreams of the one big break, which Imtiyaz Khan was in a position to provide him with.

'That is fantastic. If he has any sense, which I am sure he has in abundance, he is bound to give you a break. Let's keep our fingers crossed. Are you planning to carry your show reel? And is it updated?' His fervor had rubbed off on me as well and I had already started mentally pleading to the Gods for his success.

'Yes, the show reel is updated. And I will not be carrying it; 'We' will be carrying it with us. It is a formal, with spouse kind of a gathering and you too are coming with me.'

Imtiyaz was an acclaimed director and I knew several people who would have jumped at the thought of even setting an eye on him, let alone getting invited to a party hosted by him. I wouldn't say I wasn't excited, but strangely the more prominent emotions to emerge at the thought of attending the party were nervousness and even a tinge of fear. But the opportunity was awfully significant to permit my momentary delirium to act as an impediment. Without a thought I agreed to accompany Vishal to the party and proceeded towards the kitchen, mentally scanning my wardrobe for the right dress to wear.

'Sekhar isn't here?' I asked Vishal within minutes of entering Imtiyaz's house. The house, as expected, was a palatial four bedroom flat, with an expansive balcony that opened right into the sea. When Vishal told me about the venue, the director's residence, I had guessed that the party wouldn't be expansive, like the ones we get to see on television.

But with only about 10-12 guests - most betraying their affiliation to creative occupations with their overgrown hair, casual attire and blithe demeanor – it seemed like a much smaller and closer knit gathering. The setting was favorable from Vishal's perspective, but I couldn't help but feel out of place from the very moment we walked in. 'No, he is not coming. He had called me sometime back and said that something urgent had come up and so he would not be able to make it,' Vishal replied, depriving me of the only familiar face I could have hoped to find at the party.

Imtiyaz himself received us at the gate and ushered us in, introducing us to the other guests before offering us a seat. 'Gauri, my wife,' he said, pointing his outstretched hand towards a thickset lady adorned in a heavily embroided crepe Saree. She was wearing a halter neck blouse which was struggling to prevent parts of her from spilling out. She was fair and her features, though rounded, betrayed a lean and perhaps glorious past. 'An aftermath of comforts and luxuries that wealth begets,' I mused. She had an unmistakable haughty air about her, the kind that sends warning signals blaring in your head when you first meet such a person. Instantly I knew we weren't ever going to make the best of friends.

Imtiyaz on the other hand came across as a sensible and level-headed person. Perhaps having sensed that I was the only one in the gathering who was not connected to films, he chatted with me about my work, and to my dismay he seemed reasonably cognizant about the corporate set-up in general and the telecom sector in particular. I was impressed. He was highly affable in his conduct towards everyone, including Vishal. In fact, by the manner in which he was chatting with Vishal, no one could tell that the two had met only once before today.

Though I was slightly perplexed as to why an acclaimed director like Imtiyaz would invite us to a gathering which seemed to comprise of his closest friends and associates, I was quick to douse my reservations. The setting seemed tailor-made for Vishal and the fact was that we were sitting in Imtiyaz Khan's house, chatting with him like long lost friends, and that was all that mattered.

Alcohol was being guzzled like drops of the scanty rain showers being consumed by the arid wastelands. Our host's servant, it seemed, had orders to not let any of the glasses remain empty and hence even before a glass was completely drained, a brimming replacement could be seen sitting by its side. Soon the drinks began to have their effect and the conversation started drifting from technicalities of filmmaking to its grimy underbelly – who was sleeping with whom, which actor had exploited how many of his female leads, who all were willing to do 'anything' for a meaty role, and the likes.

The first hand gossip was fascinating to begin with but it wasn't long before the descriptions started getting liberally laced with swear words and invectives. The ladies in the group were as comfortable as the men with the debilitating language and were also contributing to it at every possible opportunity. Not that I thought of myself as a language sanitizer; in the company of friends, I can often be heard using words which, if relayed on television would have to be forcibly dubbed with a Beep. It was just that I preferred sticking to the classier epithets, refraining from using the crass and grotesque ones. And the fact that I was yet to find my zone of comfort in the alien surroundings and company was further adding to my irritation, so I quietly got up and walked out to the balcony and lit a cigarette.

In cities like Mumbai, it is only the most and the least fortunate who get a clear view of the night sky, and from where I was standing I could see not only the twinkling stars and the distant flicker of sea bound ships but also hear the calm and soothing sound of angry waves tussling against each other in a race to reach the shore. My heart was racing hither thither like a child left unattended in a gargantuan toy store. If there was a place like heaven in the whole of the city, it was right here, in Imtiyaz's balcony, and mesmerized by its magic I had lost all track of time.

I didn't know for how long I stood there staring at and soaking in the regalia of nature and it was only when I felt a hand on my shoulder that I snapped out of my trance. 'It is so lovely here, makes you forget everything, doesn't it?' I said without turning back. 'It is indeed lovely, but your silhouette makes the scenery even more enchanting,' I heard a voice from perilously close to my ears. I was startled. It wasn't Vishal's voice that I had heard. Feeling the intruder's hand on me I had assumed it to be Vishal, but I was surely mistaken. At once I turned around to find myself facing Imtiyaz, our host. He was so close to me that I could feel his whisky laced breath bouncing off my face.

Instinctively I looked over his shoulders to find the hall adorning an ambience very different from the time I had stepped out of it. The lights had been dimmed and the pitch of the music was also a tad louder. I wasn't sure, but it seemed as though some furniture had been shifted too, creating a make shift dance floor right in the centre. Three couples were clumsily moving to the beats of the music, holding and leaning on each other to support their wasted, staggering bodies. I was able to identify Mr. and Mrs. Roshan, but strangely, Mr. Roshan was dancing with the girl who had been introduced to me as Mr. Sen's fiancé. Mr. Sen on the other hand was visibly entangled with Mrs. Mehta. And wasn't that Mr. Mehta that Mrs. Roshan was cuddling up to?

My mind was refusing to process the images that my eyes were relaying. I blinked once, twice, thrice and then I realized that the hand that Imtiyaz had placed on my shoulder was still there. Sometime between then and now he had also rested his other hand on my other shoulder, and since we were facing each other, our position seemed disturbingly intimate. I couldn't step back as I could feel the railing pressing against my derriere and if I dared even a single step forward, I was bound to crash into Imtiyaz. So I tried to slide sideward, once again looking behind him in an attempt to locate my savior, Vishal.

I spotted him alright. He was sitting on the corner sofa, chatting with our hostess, clearly unaware of my precarious situation. I could not yell out to him and he wasn't looking towards me, so the prospect of him coming to my rescue was negligible, but I did find some rudimentary relief in the fact that he was only chatting with Mrs. Khan. Imtiyaz meanwhile had allowed his hands to slip, just enough so he could clasp my arms with both his hands. Then, boring into my eyes with his bloodshot ones, he said, 'You know, you should try your hand in films. You have lovely features and a fantastic body... has anyone told that to you before?'

On another day, such a compliment coming from one of the top directors of the country would have propelled me to cloud nine, but not under the given circumstances. Right now his words were sounding hollow and futile, like a used condom, washed and repackaged before being served to an unsuspecting victim for use. These lines might well have been his standard fare before taking any girl to bed, they were meaningless. The only emotion I felt was disgust and once again as I peeked behind him, I felt my loathing for everything around me shoot through the roof. I could see Mrs. Khan leaning over Vishal, bundles of her body fat resting on his thighs, chest and elsewhere, engaged in a passionate lip lock. To my utter amazement, Vishal wasn't just a silent prey; he seemed to be reciprocating as well.

'Thank you Mr. Khan, but I am not feeling too well. I think I should get going now,' I said, holding my head with one hand and blindly walking towards the hall. Thankfully Imtiyaz stepped aside at the last moment, else in my given frame of mind, I would have very easily bulldozed past him.

'Vishal,' I called out, detaching him from his passionate engagement. 'I am not feeling well. I think we should head home now,' I added.

'Why? What happened?' he said, trying to wear an expression of concern as he hesitated perceptibly before detaching himself from Gauri and springing from the sofa. 'Nothing, I have a severe headache and I am not feeling right. Let's just go home.'

'Oh dear... Why don't you lie down in one of the bedrooms for a while then? You can leave when you are feeling better,' Gauri suggested, eventually managing to pull her bulk up from the sofa. It was amazing how she could feign indifference to the fact that barely a few minutes back she was cuddling up with my husband. Her concern about my health, as it was perhaps intended to, sounded as hollow as the inside of a flute. By now some of the others too had ceased their antics and were standing around us, vainly attempting to trade the lust in their eyes for a caring expression.

'No, I think we will get going. Thanks for the offer though,' I replied sternly. 'Vishal, shall we?' I said, sifting my gaze towards my husband. My tone had a ring of certainty to it which dissuaded him from any further discussions and he quietly followed me out of the house. Not a word was spoken between us on the way back. Silently, we were both trying to settle the separate infernos of fury that were razing within us.

SEVENTEEN

The lava holed up within us started oozing as soon as we reached home and the door was shut behind us. Vishal was the first to break the silence. 'How could you do this to me?' he asked. Both of us knew that my ill health was only an extenuation and that the real reason for my insistence on an immediate exit from the party lay elsewhere.

'As if you don't know,' I shot back. Our voices were not raised as yet, but were laden with a sharp chill that was enough to slice through the sturdiest of hearts. 'I know, but I don't understand. You knew how important this party was for me; it could have paved the way for the dream break that I have been waiting for all along. And yet you decide to behave the way you did. Does my career or I for that matter, even matter to you? Or is the love that you keep proclaiming, just a feeble subterfuge?'

'I love you and so I expect you to protect me and not guide me to a pack of flesh craving hounds. You might not have problems in making out with that fat bitch, but please do it when I am not around for Gods sake. And do you even know how strongly that... that Imtiyaz was coming on to me or were you too engrossed in your own merrymaking to even notice?' I was losing control over my volume and I didn't care enough to make an attempt at checking it. The debate was baseless, preposterous at best, and Vishal looked in no mood to understand what I had to say.

'What if he was coming on to you? What would he have done? He obviously wouldn't have killed you or something. And it is not as if this is the first time that someone other than me would have touched you,' he shot back, matching my pitch. I knew that our words were now treading on hazardous frontiers, but every word that he spoke left me feeling worse than before. Instead of empathizing with me, he was justifying and almost advocating Imtiyaz's behavior and that set something ticking within me.

'So, you knew all along, didn't you? You knew that it was a party for swapping couples... and Sekhar was never expected to be there in the first place, right? Tell me... tell me...' The revelation had left me so furious that I found myself tugging at his shirt, trying to extract a reply that I desperately wanted to hear. I wanted him to tell me how I was overreacting and that it wasn't a wily trick that he had used on me. Faith, I thought, was the strongest bond that held our relationship together and if either of us had to resort to dupery and guile, it could only spell doom for us.

I was frantically shaking him, hoping for him to come clean, but instead he jerked himself away and yelled, 'Don't! Don't you dare get physical with me, I am warning you. When it comes to me, you suddenly decide to adorn a garb of chaste nobility, and what happens to this oh-I-am-so-pure self of yours when you are sleeping around with your colleagues and bosses? That… what's his name… Srinivas, yes… You can go around making out with him, that's fine, and if a man who is so important for my career decides to make a pass at you, you become too moralistic to even tolerate it. What kind of double standard is that?'

'I do what I have to, out of my own will… and if you had a problem with it, you should have said so when I told you about it. Don't forget that it was I who told you about Srini, unlike you, who sleeps around with half the girls in the city and doesn't even think it to be worth mentioning to me. You think I am blind and I don't see what is happening? Sorry to disappoint you, but I know all that transpires in the garb of your late night parties and sleep-overs. Just so you get it straight, we are husband and wife, and I am not a whore and you my pimp. Please stop expecting me to warm people's beds so that you can start getting work. And if you don't think you can get work otherwise, please sit at home; I am capable enough to run the house on my own,' I retorted. My fists were clenched, face distorted and legs trembling with fury.

'Oh, so you think I am worthless and you are the one who is running the house. Fine then, you can continue to run the house. I will figure out a way to fend for myself,' he said, storming out of the conversation and the house, slamming the door behind him. I didn't bother to stop him and neither did I feel any concern about the given hour or where he would spend whatever remained of the night. I was busy fighting a battery of demons within my own self.

Did Vishal actually love me or was our marriage simply a matter of convenience for him? The one person that I trusted blindly, how could he even try to deceive me into something so deplorable? Had I reduced myself to an entity so insignificant and frivolous that he didn't blink twice before expecting me to warm someone's bed in return for a favor? I wasn't crying, I was angry, but somewhere deep within my heart was, and the tears were incessantly pouring from my eyes.

I remember the murky light of morning seep though the curtains and the annoying croaking of crows; where have the friendly sparrows and even the disciplined roosters vanished? It must have been early morning when my brain gave up on me and against all my resistance decided to submit its exhausted self to the clutches of much needed sleep.

Late in the afternoon I opened my eyes to an angry sun and its piercing rays, a throbbing headache and a missing Vishal. He had not returned home since our argument last night. As I thought about him, the events from the party once again started to flash before my eyes and I felt a familiar needle pricking my temper. I got up and made myself some tea. I had a smoke. I flipped through some arbitrary channels on television – most relaying reruns of boring serials, showcasing the plight of their female protagonists in some obscure corner of the country or the other. 'I bet none of them ever had their husbands hustle them into sleeping with a stranger,' I thought, eventually switching off the TV.

Nothing I attempted was able to keep me from the appalling world of my thoughts and so I decided to give in. Once again I crashed on the bed, bearing the sting of my emotions – disappointment, grief, uncertainty, anger and guilt - as they converged upon me like a swarm of bees crowding their hive.

I wondered as to where I had gone wrong – whether it was in judging Vishal or in the efforts I had made towards shaping our relationship? No matter how hard I tried to attribute his behavior to a fit of anger or a momentary outburst, I was not able to convince myself to let go. Nothing could justify his act of conning me into accompanying him for the party. It was a blatant violation of my trust and that was what hurt the most.

'He could have told me before hand. We could have discussed it in advance,' I thought, quickly brushing away the idea. If Vishal had told me that it was a Swap Party we were going to, in all probability I would not have consented anyways. It would have spared me the pain of feeling betrayed, but I would still have been left wondering as to how he could even think of using my body to further his personal motives.

The driving principles of our relationship had been openness and liberty, but we forgot that a flute sounds melodious only because the air flowing through it does not gush past, but is guided by some defined constraints. Perhaps in our quest for freedom we had reduced our relationship to a sheer and flimsy existence that was incapable of holding in its folds even the basic tenets of any companionship – trust and mutual respect.

In the evening, when the sun had started to set and my pillow was soaked in my tears, I emerged from the bed once again. I wasn't succeeding in alleviating my pain. Maybe I needed someone to talk to. Someone who would listen to me, empathize with me and reassure me that all was not lost and things between Vishal and me could still return to normalcy. The only name I could think of was Kamini's.

Without bothering much about my appearance, I quickly got out of the house and started walking briskly towards Kamini's flat. As I traced the steps which, not too long back were a usual fare for me, I realized that it had been long since I had even seen my friend. She did creep up in our conversations, Vishal's and mine, once in a while but I had been so lost in my work, my home, my life, that I had been virtually ignoring her. Even the last telephonic conversation that I could recall dated back by about a fortnight. 'Maybe because I am not partying that much anymore. There are others from our old group that I haven't met in a while too,' I told myself, feebly attempting to assuage my guilt at not having kept in touch.

As I opened the main gate of the building, stepping inside, the sight ahead left me frozen stiff. Right in front of me, in the guest parking stood a shining Bullet motorcycle, one that I had gifted Vishal on our last anniversary and the installments for which were still being deducted from my salary every month. Shocked, I stood there, nailed to the spot by utter confusion and indecision.

What was Vishal doing here? Is this where he had been since last night? A fresh set of questions started ringing in my head, but this time I found a possible medium to satisfy some of them – the security guard of the building. He knew me as an erstwhile resident and when I checked with him about the time since when the motorcycle was parked inside the building, he replied unhesitatingly. 'It wasn't here last evening, but when I came for my duty today morning at about 7.00, it was here and it hasn't moved ever since. But why do you ask madam?' he replied. I didn't wait to give him an answer and instead traced my steps back to my house. I had a vague feeling that I knew the implications of this, one that I was desperately trying to suppress.

Vishal did not come home on Sunday night either. The knowledge of his whereabouts had only worsened my condition and I could feel another tendon in my temple throbbing rapidly. Kamini was my childhood friend. Why then had Vishal chosen to seek refuge in her flat? And moreover why did she agree to entertain him? Agreed, he was her friend too, but wasn't he her childhood friend's husband first? Shouldn't she have checked with him as to why he was knocking on her door at such an unearthly hour? And if she did, what explanations had Vishal given her? Vishal had fought with me, but why didn't she call to inform me about his whereabouts? If she knew about our fight, why didn't she even bother to check on me? It was a day of unanswered questions and I had just added a fresh bunch to the already long list.

I was a heightened case of Monday morning blues when I walked into office the next morning, deprived of sleep and mental peace. My mind though, in its state of overdrive, amid a lot of nonsense, had come up with a jewel of a thought to settle another fraction of the blanket of curiosity I was shrouded by. I settled quickly, logging into the system, browsing through my inbox for any urgent mails, before heading back towards the lobby. My destination, the customer service department, was located on the floor above ours and I opted for the staircase instead of waiting for the lift to take me there.

By a stroke of luck, both Vishal and Kamini were on my company's mobile network. Each action of theirs in the mobile space passed through a complex set of company systems and was duly recorded for the purpose of billing. The employees in the customer service department had access to customer account screens whereby they could view itemized, billed and unbilled information pertaining to the mobile usage by any customer on the network. I walked up to the floor manager, a lady that I had often seen in the office but other than a few passing smiles, never had the opportunity to interact with.

I introduced myself and requested her to help me with latest itemized bills for the two numbers I scribbled on a pad on her desk. 'The numbers belong to my husband and another friend; both their bills seem to have got misplaced,' I explained. The lady did not have any reason to be alarmed and within minutes I was on the way back to my desk, duplicate copies of both bills in my hands.

As I settled back on my seat, I couldn't help but smile at my own stupidity. All I wanted to check were the calls made to or received from any one of their numbers to or from the other, and I didn't need both bills for that purpose; any one bill would have sufficed.

Waving aside the fleeting guilt I felt towards the innocent trees that had been felled for producing the paper I had just wasted due to my callousness, I opened the duplicate bill for Vishal's number.

It was a twelve page document with the listing of numbers segregated in separate sections for received calls, calls made and text messages, and an initial flip-through revealed that my suspicions were not totally unfounded and that Kamini's number was indeed featuring there at an alarming regularity. I then got down to a detailed analysis, circling her number wherever it appeared, analyzing the time and duration of the call and trying to recall as to which day from our lives had that been – a task that took me over a hour and half. But by the end of it I had startling facts to support the hypothesis that a part of me had been hoping to be incorrect.

There wasn't a day when Vishal and Kamini had not spoken at least a couple of times, the average call duration being anywhere between twenty to twenty five minutes. In fact on some days they had spoken for as many as six to seven times and their longest conversation on record had been for 126 minutes. I couldn't remember the last time that Vishal and I had chatted for that long even in person, let alone over the phone. Most calls had been made during the day, when I was expectedly slogging at work. There also were the few odd calls made at peculiar hours of the night – all made by Vishal, on days that he had supposedly been out partying or when I had retired early.

I wasn't left in a state to get much work done in whatever remained of the day, so I asked Srini to be excused for the second half and headed home. Sitting in the auto I found myself searching for reasons, other than the obvious one that was staring me in the face, to explain the information I had unearthed, and I found myself faring miserably.

'Kamini… Wasn't she the one who had counseled me into getting married to Vishal? And wasn't she the friend who, to me, had always been the sister I never had? How could she do such a thing? And Vishal, the man I had devoted my whole life to, he couldn't find any other girl in the whole of Mumbai, but Kamini?' I was the hapless victim, the tormented, and tragically enough, my tormentors were those very people I had considered to be my own. I could feel my life being crushed under the burden of my misery, just as God knows how many unsuspecting insects would be getting squashed under the wheels of the racing auto.

EIGHTEEN

I spotted Vishal's bike parked in its usual parking spot below our flat. He was finally home, but instead of relief I found myself grappling with an inexplicable hesitation. There were too many things on my mind and I needed time to sort them out. The last thing I wanted was a confrontation with him. Instead of ringing the doorbell, I used my set of keys to unlock the door and entered the house.

He was there, comfortably perched on a beanbag, watching television. He greeted me with a deliberate indifference, not sifting his gaze to even acknowledge my arrival, and I was glad. I went about my usual chores, reciprocating his coldness and made myself a cup of tea before picking up a book and heading towards the bedroom. I didn't bother to ask if he too wanted some tea.

With time my agony, instead of subsiding, had only shifted tracks. I realized that I was no longer thinking about Imtiyaz or Gauri or the events from the party that had led to it all. The party, it now seemed, was only the tip of the iceberg and actually it was a much deeper evil that had slowly but surely been eating into the fabric of my marriage, catching me completely off guard. Had it been only the party, there was an outside chance that I would have forgiven Vishal, and but for a few scars, we could even have made up by now. After all hadn't I ceased thinking about that episode already? But this was different. I had been cheated and both people who I thought to be my own had joined hands in this deceit. The feeling was beyond forgiveness or absolution.

We shared the same roof – Vishal and I - we even slept on the same bed, but as two complete strangers, just like two fellow travelers sharing a train berth. We didn't speak, we avoided being caught looking at each other and neither of us made any attempts to break the ice. The house we had put together so painstakingly had been robbed of its soul and felt like a lifeless corpse, the inanimate furniture and accessories making up its now defunct organs. It was as though we had both left our relationship to be ravaged by the minute, tearing destruction of time.

I heard Vishal use his phone a couple of times and despite my best efforts I found myself straining my ears to catch the words that were being exchanged. Was he speaking with Kamini? What was he telling her? What kind of tone he used while talking to her?

The first call had been too hushed, further elevating my curiosity levels, and the second was to a nearby restaurant that we sometimes ordered food from. I heard Vishal order for two wraps – enough only to serve as his dinner - and later when I felt the need I made myself a pack of Maggie noodles. Something significant had snapped within our relationship and from such close quarters the damage seemed irreparable.

As is common knowledge, all mobile service providers possess the functionality of listening in to conversations that pass through their network and ours was no different. Only, to prevent any violation of customer privacy, the orders for such phone tapping operations usually percolated from the highest levels within the organizational hierarchy, often at the behest of one of the law enforcement agencies.

Having spent a considerable amount of time in the telecom sector, I was well aware of this possibility and in it I saw a medium to not only address my lingering doubts about my understanding of the situation but also provide me with some concrete evidence for whatever path I chose thereon – confronting Vishal, being forewarned about his next move, or who knows what.

And so, the next morning, I found myself walking towards Srini's cabin with a steely resolve in my mind. If there was any one person in the entire company who had the wherewithal to help me, it was him, and I was prepared to scale any lengths to get him to agree to this one request of mine.

The task didn't turn out to be as tedious as I had imagined. As soon as I started narrating the story of Vishal's unfaithfulness, my tears started to flow uncontrollably. It wasn't something I had planned. Perhaps because it was the first time I had the opportunity to voice my plight to a third person, my tears too decided to make their presence felt. It worked to my advantage though and a visibly moved Srini was soon sending out mails, arranging for all calls between the two specified numbers to be recorded and shared with him. I am sure he realized the risk he was subjecting himself to, and I found myself overwhelmed at the gesture. It had been a while since someone had gone out of his or her way for the sake of my happiness.

The machination was in place and while Vishal and I continued surviving under one roof – two erstwhile companions, making an attempt to salvage some dignity out of their forced cohabitation through unfamiliarity and indifference - every evening I found myself in Srini's cabin, listening to the conversations that had been stealthily recorded over the past twenty four hours.

It took barely the first few sentences of their first conversation eavesdropped on to establish the truth behind my worst fears. It weren't the 'darlings', 'sweethearts' and other questionable nomenclatures they were freely using to address each other or their honey soaked voices, but something within my own self that revealed the truth behind what I was listening. As soon as I heard Vishal's voice I knew that I had lost him to Kamini, an instinct that emerged from the three long years that we had spent as man and wife. But it was only on the third day of my snooping that I hit the goldmine, or should I call it a blossoming growth of poison ivy?

For your benefit, I am reproducing the snippets from their conversation that I can recall now.

Vishal:	Hey Sweetheart!
Kamini:	Hi. So, you finally got the time to call?
Vishal:	No yaar, was meaning to call you as soon as I got up, but got held up with another call. And wait till…

Kamini (Cutting him short): I knew you would be ready with your excuses. And what about last night, why didn't you call then?

Vishal: Last night was all thanks to your friend, so don't blame me. I waited a long time for her to sleep, but she didn't. She seems to have turned into an insomniac…

Kamini: You know what your problem is; you are too soft from the inside. If everything is over between you two, why are you still scared to call me in front of her? Why can't you simply tell her about us and ask for a divorce? She is my friend too, but I don't keep fretting over what she will think or how she will react when she finds out about us. I am fine with coming out in the open and if she understands, great, and if not, well, too bad. Why can't you too be upfront and straight about your feelings with her?

Vishal: It isn't that easy when you have spent so much time with someone. She is not in the right frame of mind and God knows how she will react if I ask her for a divorce as of now. Just bear with me for a few more days and as soon as the time is opportune, I will have a word with her.

Kamini: Promise?

Vishal: Of course! But forget that and listen to the news I have for you…

Kamini: What?

Vishal: We are getting another chance… Can you believe that? Gauri called a little while back. I explained all that has transpired in my life since I last met her and I also told her about you. And guess what, she has asked us to come over for dinner today.

Kamini (Though excited, but evidently not as much as Vishal): Wow, that's great news. So, are we going there then?

Vishal: Obviously, we are, unless of course you are having second thoughts about your decision. And if that is the case, tell me, and we can still back out.

Kamini: Are you crazy? Why would you even think of something like that? I am not like her that I will cling on to some false sense of morality and deprive you of what could be a chance of a lifetime. I can do anything for you Vishal.

Vishal: Oh… you are so sweet. It is entirely my fault, you were always there and yet I failed to see you in the correct light…

Kamini (Once again cutting him short):	Stop it, will you? Even I didn't look at you in that fashion earlier, else why would I have cajoled you two to get together? But bygones are bygones, why fret over them? Let's look at the brighter side of things. We will be together soon, won't we?
Vishal:	Yes, we will be, and I can't wait for that day to arrive.

'Ma, one more Thepla please. You don't know how much I missed them,' I said, barely pausing to look up from my plate. She came up behind me and placed another one of her delicious Theplas on my plate. 'Eat, my baby, eat all that you want. We all missed you too,' she said, lovingly stroking my hair.

I felt my tears wetting my cheeks once again. 'Ma, I have been such a bad daughter. I have troubled you and papa so much…,' I said, breaking into a sob.

'Na beta, don't cry. You have done nothing wrong. All of us make mistakes in our lives, nobody is perfect. What is important is to learn from them and emerge from our problems as stronger and wiser beings, and that is what you have done my child. We are both very proud of you,' I heard my father's voice. I hadn't seen him enter the room, but he had obviously heard my dialogue with my mother and was now standing next to my chair, patting my back.

I couldn't see my mother's face at all and my father too was barely visible, so I tried to get up from the dining table to turn and face them. It had been so long, I wanted to see them, touch them, hug them, but in all my excitement, some part of me caught the plate and it came crashing down to the floor from the dining table. The noise from the falling plate was loud enough to wake any sleeping soul and I found myself rubbing my eyes too.

I was on my bed, the bed in my Mumbai flat. I wasn't in Rajkot and my parents were nowhere in sight. Just then I heard another noise from the kitchen, like someone searching for a vessel, rummaging through the entire utensil rack. I looked up at the wall clock – 6.00 a.m. Vishal had returned home and was probably trying to make himself a cup of tea.

I allowed my thoughts to drift back in time to last evening when I had returned from office. Vishal was not home as usual. I knew exactly where he was and what he was up to, but that hardly had any bearings on my situation. I was still trying to come to terms with the conversation between him and Kamini that I was now privy to, and some of my unanswered questions had come back to hound me once again. Why did Kamini do this to me, and why Vishal? Where did I go wrong?

Without bothering about food, I had headed to the bedroom and lit a cigarette. I had a lot of thinking to do. I knew that the mirage called marriage was over for me and I had to arrive at the crucial decision about what to do with rest of my life. But before I could shift my attention to the future, I had my past waiting to be deciphered, for the sake of my own sanity. I was bogged down by the multitude of unanswered questions that continued to hound me, prohibiting any efforts on my part to come to terms with the reality of my life.

Perhaps it was the quest for freedom and the dazzle of the unknown that drew me away from my home. But that couldn't have been the mistake for which I was paying so dearly. There were enough examples of people around me who had stepped out of their homes to pursue their ambitions and none of them was faced with a situation as grave and gloomy as mine. Surely it must have been some other mistake, one that I had unknowingly committed in the pursuit of my own dreams, that was now looming over my head like an ominous cloud.

But then, what was the dream I had been chasing all along? I had no dreams. And maybe it was just that, the absence of a dream that did me in. I allowed myself to flow unchecked with each enticement that presented itself in my path and eventually found myself adrift in a zone that I hadn't been groomed to tackle. The world I had knowingly chosen was alien to me and perhaps it was the frustration of not being able to find my footing, given the shackles of my ingrained values that drew me further and further from the reality I had wished to embrace.

My mistake perhaps was that I was still seeking real-world emotions, warmth and relationships in a world of illusions and frivolity that I had been unknowingly residing in. I failed to recognize its business-like character, where deals have replaced relationships and emotions are subservient to practicality. In my naivety I had made myself vulnerable to inflictions of the kind that I eventually was being made to bear. The remote and vague suspicion that had dawned upon me on seeing Vishal's bike parked under Kamini's apartment had become a concrete and dramatic reality of my life.

I recalled Kamini having told me some time back that her folks too were hounding her to get married. I don't know how, perhaps because unlike my parents they had arrived at a compromise with their daughter's outlook towards life, but they had agreed to accept a groom of her choice, caste, creed or religion not withstanding. She, despite being the beacon to steer me away from my past life, had managed to strike a balance between her own past and present. Who knows, maybe Vishal too was an arrangement, an easy and convenient option for her to retain this balance – appeasing her parents by taking the marital plunge while retaining her current lifestyle in its basal form. Only the right choice of partner could have made this work for her and Vishal fit the bill to perfection. But even if that was the case, what was wrong with it? Wasn't she herself a matter of convenience for Vishal?

The more I thought about my predicament, the more justifications I found for Vishal's and Kamini's actions, leaving only myself to bear the burden of blame. I didn't know what to do or where to go. In my impulsiveness and vain sense of vanity I had mercilessly severed my ties with my parents – sending them a card to inform them of my wedding - an act I could not even hope to be forgiven. No, going back home was not an option. I was a different girl from the one who had once lived in that quaint and sleepy town. I was a girl who had lived a tabooed life in Mumbai – drinking, smoking, sleeping with countless men - and not to mention the tattoo that was still clinging to my chest like a scalding reminder of all things I shouldn't have done. Hell, I wasn't even Sejal anymore; I was Sherlyn Ahuja, a girl that the city of Rajkot did not even recognize.

These were the thoughts in the midst of which I had slipped into deep sleep sometime not very long ago. As I pulled myself out of the bed now, I suddenly felt a lot lighter in the head and much surer about myself than I had ever felt lately. The dream had come to me like a guiding light and suddenly I knew what I was going to do with my crumbling life.

Parents are known to be forgiving and ever-loving, especially when it came to their offsprings, concordant or wayward. I had been bad, real bad, but if there was anyone I could turn to at such a delicate juncture of my life, it had to be them. Maybe it was time that I ended my big-city honeymoon and left the world I had created around me for the one I had heartlessly deserted. And maybe my parents still loved me enough to accept me back, an erring offspring who had learnt from her mistakes.

I knew that my honeymoon with Mumbai had ended and there was no point in hanging on to the dilapidated shreds from my past life. I couldn't allow myself to be consumed by insidious traps of grief, vengeance or even nostalgia. I needed peace, solace and sympathy, I needed to be loved and cared for, and more importantly I needed to restore my lost faith in human relationships. The dream had cleared the clouds of indecision from my head and I knew where the answers to all my problems lay. It was only in the comforting presence of my parents, my father's tender embrace and my mother's affectionate words, that I could gather the strength to reconstruct my derelict existence.

Once I knew what I had to do, pack my bags and head to Rajkot, the unanswered questions that had been hammering me from within were quick to settle. Suddenly it didn't matter as to why Vishal or Kamini had done what they did. It was all too inconsequential now. As if the questions were mushrooming purely out of my own confusion and uncertainty, only to vanish as soon as clarity dawned upon me. Though I was slightly nervous at the thought of my parent's reaction at my unexpected arrival after all these days, I was eager, nearly desperate, to get back home. I needed to get down to packing my bag, but before that there was another matter I needed to tend to.

I was not going to allow Vishal the pleasure of calling off our marriage. He was the one who had strayed, and if anything, I deserved the right to sound the death knell of our relationship. With determined steps and a steely resolve in my eyes I headed towards the kitchen for the final confrontation with Vishal, one that was long overdue.